Son of the Fallen

A Novel

By ALAN T. LUU

The first in the
SON OF THE FALLEN Series

ISBN: 0984875913
ISBN-13: 978-0984875917

Dedicated to Veronika -
for all your loving support.
This is to our new, glorious
adventure together.

TABLE OF CONTENTS

"They were the heroes of old,
men of renown."

Prologue

Forty Years in the Mojave Desert

IN THE BEGINNING, James Henry Worth had howled like a dog. Before, he had never suffered as much as an abrasion on his rhinoceros-like skin.

They flew in leisurely, and he would see them, two specks in the low sky, for what seemed like hours until they approached and landed upon his shoulders. They made no sound, but he could see the hunger in their eyes. His body used to buck and convulse in pain, his arms wrenching against his manacles, his wrists tearing at the iron until it was raw. But after decades of being chained to a desert rock and tortured, he bore the feedings in silence, losing consciousness, waking sometimes long after the metallic beaks had ravished his insides.

The two condors, one albino in color, with red eyes and blood-colored splotches on her chest, the other, black and muscular, with blue sun-tipped feathers, came once a week during the heat of the day. They started with his eye lids, peeling them off slowly, one at a time, as if enjoying an appetizer. His sockets remained untouched, perhaps so he could witness their relish of the main course—his torso. He never had the chance to ask. Never had the *Why* answered that exploded in his brain every time they feasted on his gut.

1

He would heal during the days after their weekly visits. His intestines would reform. The thin linings of subcutaneous and visceral fat would regenerate. The robust strands of his abdominal and oblique muscles would rejuvenate themselves. Severed blood vessels and nerves would regrow, according to the near-perfect design of his formidable genetic code. But, those condors would always return.

Zack and Charlotte. He had named them after two cousins. When he was eight years old, he met these cousins, twins, for the first and only time. One was a girl, Charlotte, with bright red hair and a small pointed nose. The boy, Zachary, had long black hair which covered his eyes. They played hide and seek, and Charlotte insisted on being "it" every time. She would find James, every time, with no hesitation, whether he had gone up to the attic, down to the basement, or whether he went into his secret place in the backyard—the hollow of a lightning-scorched tree.

Each time she found him, Charlotte would pinch an ear with her long, red fingernails and pull him out. After an hour of this, an exasperated Zachary threw James in the trash bin, and then hid himself under a pile of leaves and a dead possum. She still found them almost immediately. She declared her boredom, and leaning in towards James, who was sitting in the trash bin, she whispered that she no longer wanted to play with a "slut's son." His two cousins then walked away. By the time he came back to the house, they were gone, and he never saw them again.

Now, chained bare-chested under the desert sun, James was invisible to the drivers on the highway that was a hundred fifty yards away, the California Highway Patrol, and passing sparrows alike. Even though Zack and Charlotte always found him for their weekly spectacle, in between those visits were endless days of dry, mind-numbing heat.

During the intervening years of his confinement, he started keeping count of the trucks that would occasionally roar upon the runaway truck ramp, his ramp, fifty-five miles past Barstow along the 15 Interstate. Here, the road sloped downwards as it headed north. A ramp was constructed to the side of the northbound lanes, piled with small river stones—a fail-safe for semi-trailer trucks with bad brakes.

James was chained high on a peculiar tower of rock, east of the ramp. He eyed each automobile that came from the south, checking to see if he could find the telltale wobbling of tires, or hear the frantic honking of the driver. Shivers would shoot up his spine, in that rare moment when a truck crashed onto the ramp and sent plumes of angry dust and pebbles flying. It was one of his only amusements while chained to the sunbaked rock formation.

The first few years, he often wept. The emptiness was crushing. He would open his eyes and weep upon seeing the empty highway, its lines blurred by the Mojave heat. He would close his eyes and be confronted with the remnants of some horrible nightmare. But, night after night of despair chiseled away his ability to feel the pain. The tremendous sun dried his tears upon his cheek, and eventually no drops fell from his face.

He learned to slip into his memories. He tread where his consciousness would lead him, obsessing over some details and letting his mind indulge itself, while other things faded away and were nearly forgotten. Certain memories were still clear as the desert sky, while others were now sunken beneath the sand. But, one thing he would never forget was the Minotaur.

It came and took him from his backyard one summer night in 1963. His mother, Emilia, had allowed him to sleep in the hammock, and he had been gazing at the stars, marveling at the clashes of titans in the sky. At the age of seventeen, James was already tall and muscled, a large man with a boy's face. But the Minotaur was larger, a beast with a bull's face. It had come at midnight, descending upon the backyard on a cloud, a naked monstrosity with ivory spikes protruding from its shoulders and upper arms.

The dark cloud came and blocked the sky theater, and before the sleepy teenager had realized what was going on, the largest eyes he had ever seen were staring into his own. Enormous nostrils spouted steam across his face. He started to shout to his mother, asleep in the house, but the Minotaur had covered his face with a massive palm. It bear hugged James, and as his body went limp, the Minotaur threw him across the yard. Hitting the ground, James had one last thought before losing consciousness—*hooves?*

James had woken up some time later in a dank stone cell. Once his eyes adjusted to the dark, he called out for his mother, but only heard the echo of his voice. Then, a naked woman came to the bars of his cell. He was stunned by her ethereal beauty, but soon, he noticed that this violet-eyed woman had no legs. From her hips, her flawless skin transitioned into scales that matched the color of her eyes. She was a snake below her waist, her tail trailing into the dark shadows behind her.

Upon her forehead, a great red stone was embedded, a faint light throbbing within. In a daze, he allowed her to lead him to another room that contained contraptions made of brown, rusted metal, and many ropes and leather straps. She tethered him by his wrists and ankles on a wooden table, and then fingered through a crate of tools with rotted wooden handles. She selected one with glee in her eyes and turned to where he lay. But the woman-serpent had underestimated him. He was distracted and confused, but James was still quite strong. When she attempted to cut him with a brown, rusted machete, he broke his leather fetters without much effort. Screaming and flailing his arms to keep her away, he knocked the creature dead in the skull and ran from the room.

By the time the Minotaur came to the scene, the red stone in her brow still ebbed gently, but Echidna was breathless, her eyes a dull gray, and James was long gone.

James staggered for weeks through a wilderness. He faintly remembered following a stream and drinking from its cool water.

He found himself in a small town, rambling incoherently, and somehow, he ended up in the bed of a truck, mostly sleeping as it made its way along a winding coastal highway. Sometime later, James awoke. His clothes were torn and brown from dirt, his hair crusted and gnarled, and he was sprawled underneath his hammock.

Crashing through the back door of his house, he yelled once again for his mother. In the kitchen, he found someone else waiting for him. She was an older woman he had never seen before. She dressed in a beige, well-ironed blouse, tapered brown dress pants, clasped around the waist by a belt of gold. Her white hair was tied tightly in a bun. As she walked up to him, he could see in her eyes a rage and passion unlike any he had ever seen.

"Look at you," she said. "Miserable, dirty boy. Running and running—doing no good for anybody, including yourself." With her head cocked to the side, and her lips clenched, she examined his face. "You look too much like your father."

"I don't know my father," he said automatically.

It was true. His mother never mentioned his father.

"Who are you?" James had asked the woman.

She slapped him with a lightning-quick hand, and equally quickly she fingered a dark paste out of a small jar and smeared some on his forehead, and then his cheeks. He stared straight into her eyes—cold and ice-blue.

"I'm the lady of dreams, you bastard-child," she finally whispered as she clasped his painted face in both hands. "For you, I have reserved very dark dreams. I am your father's rightful, honored wife. And I deserve justice."

A sensation of falling overcame him, and he could not resist closing his eyes. Now, after an endless procession of seasons chained to a rock, he could barely remember that long, horrid dream. All he could remember, mostly, was the Minotaur—the snarling, unheavenly rage of its bull-face. And hooves. It really did have hooves for feet. Heavy, bloody hooves.

5

Chapter 1

A Stranger Alters Fate

SOMETIME IN THE WINTER, James had lost consciousness. It happened now and then, for no specific reason. He often teetered on the edge of cognizance, and sometimes he would fall away, deeply. He woke up periodically through the spring, now and then during Zack and Charlotte's visits, which were occurring haphazardly in recent years. Sometimes he woke up to nothing but a gentle breeze on his face. Then he would fall to sleep again.

Now, summer had arrived. The leathering of his skin under the fiery sun made that clear. His arms, torso, and most of his legs, all exposed to the sweltering heat, were tanned a deep brown. His long hair was caked with desert sand and covered much of his face as his head hung low.

In recent days, he started to feel more lucid. He had been almost *eager* for some unknown reason. He often lifted his head, shifting his gaze from the sand below to the runaway truck ramp. For years now, it had remained disused.

Out of a quiet desperation, he started to count the red station wagons that passed by on the highway. He was at two. He had long ago dropped the habit of counting sunrises and sunsets. But his body ached, and his belly itched. More than a few weeks had passed since Zack and Charlotte last appeared, and they were long overdue for arrival.

He took a break from staring at the highway and looked toward the northeast. A single Joshua tree stood out of normal eyesight range, but James could see it. With its branches extending skyward, it looked to him like a hand that had burst up from underground, reaching desperately skyward for help. Mormon settlers who had crossed the Mojave Desert more than a century earlier had named these trees after the prophet Joshua, because they looked like a man standing with his arms raised towards the heavens.

His eyes lazily diverted back to the road in time to see another red station wagon arrive upon the horizon. It was the third. It was coming from the southwest, from Barstow, and was going slow for this strip of highway. His attention became fixed on the car, his only distraction perhaps for the rest of the day. As it came closer, cruising on the downward slope of the road, he could see that it was slowing more. It had nearly eased to a crawl when the driver did a very curious thing. The car sped up, and approaching the ramp, it swerved off to the side and up the ramp, sending the requisite cloud of chaos all around.

The car settled near the top, and once the dust cleared, the driver opened the door and came out. James could see that it was probably a man, dressed in a dark suit. He reached back into his car, brought something out, and put it to his face. Then, he looked out into the desert. After several minutes, the man walked to the back of the car and pulled something out the backdoor. He unfolded what looked like a wheelchair and pushed it carefully as he came down the ramp. *Odd.*

The man spent a good amount of time wandering the desert space between the highway and James. He would push to the east, then the south, stopping here and there to pull some type of contraption out of his bag and surveying the area. Finally, when he was about fifty yards away, the man looked straight at James, and then he bagged his device and started to push the wheelchair at the rock formation.

A few minutes later, the man, who was now at the very bottom of the rock, thirty feet below, was shuffling through his bag once again. He was not very tall, lithe, in a blue pinstriped suit. He had blond hair that was slicked back, eyeglasses, and a small mustache that marked an otherwise young-looking face. He pulled out a pickaxe, and a flask, then approached the bottom of the rock tower. Without even taking off his jacket, the man slammed the pickaxe overhead into the stone and started to climb up.

He was quite agile, in a little boy sort of way, and made good progress up the tower, finally making it to just below James's feet. The man had been feeling about as he climbed, and now, he was groping about in earnest. To James's surprise, he grasped at one of the chains that wrapped from the back of the rock. He held on with both hands and, using the chain as leverage, pulled himself around to the other side.

James could no longer see the man, but he felt the chains tugging against his torso, arms, and legs. He could also hear the man grunting as he struggled. James then heard a very violent, sizzling sound. The chains around his legs started loosening, and then falling, below him. His legs swung free. Then, the chains around his torso unraveled, and as they fell, he could see the ends were melted off. All that was left to hold James up were the chains clamped to his wrists, and even then, more sizzling sounds came from behind him. James was suddenly loose, his stomach lurched, and he fell thirty feet to the desert ground.

He was facedown and half-buried in sand. A large stone dug sharply into his thigh, and he could do nothing about it. The fiery pain throbbed in his leg, but he could not move a muscle. Then, he heard the man shuffling around him, and he was pulled by his shoulder onto his back. He stared straight up at black-rimmed glasses and a blond patchy mustache.

"Oh, you're conscious!" the man shouted.

James said nothing. He became aware of how dry his mouth felt, as if it was filled with cobwebs that also fastened it shut.

"Oh, well, you might want to give it a little time with the talking bit," the man said. "You are *quite* out of practice." He gave an awkward laugh. He ran to the wheelchair and hauled it back to James. "Sorry about that fall, but I was told you could handle it, ha-ha," he said. "You are immortal, correct? Or half? Is semi-immortal the correct term? Ha-ha!"

The skinny man was able to pull him into the wheelchair after some time. He was wiry thin and approximately a foot shorter than James, who still had no control over his body. He could move his fingers slightly, but his head rolled back and forth as they made their way back toward the road. Meanwhile, the man grunted and groaned, struggling to get the wheelchair over the rocky terrain.

After some time, he was able to get James to the base of the ramp. He then climbed the ramp back up to the red car. James was disappointed that the car didn't look exactly like a station wagon. It was similar to the station wagon, a car that was a favorite of his as a young boy, yet shorter, with a round rear. It was an egg of a car.

As he waited in the wheelchair, his thoughts strayed to when he was a teenager and had taken trips to Santa Monica or Malibu, down the California coast from his home in Goleta. He would watch the surfers. At the time, everyone emulated "The Man Who Could Walk on Water," George Freeth, and Duke Kahanamoku, the legendary Hawaiian. His favorite car was the woody surf car that many of them transported their long boards on, along with their cargo of hamburger patties and towels.

James snapped back to the present as the blond man backed his car off the ramp, and sand and rock flew into his face. It was working fine. Soon, they were on the highway. Wheelchair and mysterious bag stowed away in the car's cramped backseat, the man drove north on the 15, proceeded to exit at the next road, and then turned back around on the southbound. As the car approached eighty miles per hour, James's vision blurred. The forward momentum caused a dizzy spell. It took the next few miles before he adjusted to the motion.

"You know, those years in the desert sun would have killed a mortal man, but you look relatively healthy, albeit a bit sunburnt, ha-ha," chuckled the man, as he drove on. He drove calmly, two hands gripping the wheel. A large jade ring adorned his left hand. "You know, I come from a special lineage myself. One of the advantages of my ancestry is that I can function in pretty much any weather. Neither cold nor heat affects me much."

After a while, houses started appearing on either side of the highway, and the man once again exited the highway, using an off ramp with a sign advertising the Barstow Outlet Mall. Cruising down Lenwood Road, James couldn't help but notice all the signs, huge signs that spanned the length of entire buildings, all along the road. A tremendous amount of wires crisscrossed the street and over the structures, connected here and there by tall brown wooden poles that were like trees with foliage of wire and metal boxes. They existed in the cities and towns of his childhood, but James never noticed them like he did now, dominating the landscape and zigzagging the horizon. James closed his eyes and hung his head. A headache was beginning to sinuate into his brain. The motion and visual stimuli started to overwhelm him.

They pulled into the parking lot of the Good Nite Motel, and the man left the car for a few minutes. When he came back, he parked it in front of #103 and was soon struggling to drag James, without wheelchair, into the motel room and onto the bed. It was more of the same as before—banter, grunt, laugh, banter, grunt, laugh. He made sure that the curtains were closed, then said, "Cheerio, I'll be back in the morning," and was promptly gone, leaving James in the darkened room alone.

Lying on the bed, with its clean crisp sheets tucked in between the mattresses and frame, James felt the soft textures beneath his back, arms, and legs. He forced himself to stay awake for a minute, savoring the unexpected freedom from his prison. He caressed the cotton comforter beneath him. His calloused palms traced across the delicate fabric in small circles as he tried to hang on to consciousness. But soon, he was fast asleep. His eyes were bolted shut. His limbs were splayed across the king-size bed, and, for the first time in many years, he snored, the rising and falling of his amplified breathing audible even to those walking by outside his room.

Chapter 2

Briallen Davies

EVEN AT SEVEN YEARS OLD, Briallen Davies was allowed by her mother and father to roam throughout their town of Aberaeron, from the Tabernacle Chapel, on to the busy port, then back to the green field on the edge of town that was a stone's throw from her backyard. Briallen would often play by herself, bringing along her drawings of deer, birds, and other creatures that were, in Briallen's eyes, supernatural, and also her favorite toy, a kite that her Aunt Alis had given her for her seventh birthday.

Briallen had learned with all certainty from Aunt Alis that King Arthur himself had once been led by a white deer to Sir Pellinore's well, in the land of magic. Her field was surrounded by tall elm trees, with Georgian houses along its perimeter, and families could often be found there, picnicking or running with their dogs. These families would often see a little girl there, holding out her drawings in front of her, as they led her from tree to tree, searching for a doorway to Sir Pellinore's well.

On one such occasion in the middle of spring, while running in her field, a strong gust of wind blew Briallen's drawings out of her hands. She chased them all, making no progress, as she was constantly turning to and fro, first grasping at one sheet, then the other. All the while, she tried to hang on to her kite, its string rolled and wrapped around her arm. But she finally settled on one, her favorite drawing of a deer she had once seen in the Aeron Valley, and chased it through the elms. Upon catching it, Briallen saw that she had stumbled upon a Hawthorn bush, in the midst of the tall elms, that she had not seen before. It was more than a bush. It had grown to be a fairly large tree in itself, and on its branches were striking pink blossoms.

The young girl stood and stared, as she was in the habit of doing whenever she saw something she had never seen before. She noticed that the leaves and blossoms were moving vigorously, more vigorously than the wind could have been blowing. So she walked up close, right underneath the shadow of the tree, and looked up into its boughs. Sure enough, she could see that someone was up in the tree, perhaps a boy, perhaps a man, and that he was collecting the blossoms into a basket, his darting hands moving quicker than she could track. She called up into the tree, with her curious, squeaky voice. Immediately, the person in the tree froze, his fingers just about to pluck another blossom from its place. As quickly as he had stopped, he darted from his place, seemingly climbing higher up the branches, and then he was gone from sight.

Briallen waited for several hours, whistling an old tune, clutching onto both her kite and drawing. When it was time to go—her mother and father did want her back in time for supper—Briallen was hesitant to leave. She did not want to lose her new tree. So, as any curious seven-year-old girl who chased magical deer would do, she decided to dig a little hole and bury her drawing, with her kite along with it, at the base of the Hawthorn, making sure not to bury the kite's line. She then left her new tree, holding onto the string as tightly as possible. Briallen did not know how long she wandered, and she did not find it strange that she never ran out of string, but she eventually came to the edge of her field. Walking up to an elm tree she recognized, she tied the end of the kite string around the base of the tree. There was just enough length for it.

Briallen of course returned the next day. She found the elm and then followed her string trail all the way back to the Hawthorn. She did not find it surprising that the Hawthorn was stripped of all its blossoms, its branches looking quite ordinary. For years afterwards, usually in the spring, Briallen would return to her Hawthorn tree, looking for the boy she had seen in its boughs. Sometimes, she would find it full of its pink blossoms, and in those moments she admired the beauty of her tree. But more often than not, she would find it stripped of its pink ornaments, and she always knew who had done it.

Years passed, and Briallen came to almost forget her tree, as life's injuries took its toll. The biggest blows came when she was sixteen—the deaths of her parents in a boating accident in the harbor. But Briallen went along, and she lived in the family house by herself, often visiting her Aunt Alis, who lived in Cardigan down the coast. She was still quiet, tall and graceful, with golden hair down to her waist. She had outgrown her drawings, but now she wrote in her journal, crafting pages of words that had poured out of her mind about hidden forests, mysterious beings, and things unknown. Although young men often turned their eyes to her and called for her attention with their own sweet words, she paid them little attention and did not write of them in her journal.

On the day after her eighteenth birthday, she decided it was time to visit the Hawthorn again. She desired change. Spring had come, still in its early weeks. She found her string, mostly buried but still tied to the elm tree. She followed it and was pleased to once again discover the Hawthorn still with bloom. She had a large basket, and spending the whole morning and afternoon, Briallen collected all the pink blossoms herself.

The boy, or rather he was a man now, came to the tree a few days later, and he found the branches of the Hawthorn empty of its treasure. But upon the edge of the clearing, a single blossom sat upon the ground, and as he went to collect it, he found another blossom, several yards further. Soon, his basket was half-full, and he went through the groves, collecting the Paul's Scarlet, as he knew it was called. One by one, the blossoms led him out of the elms, and along a small path, he found himself behind a house that was old and gorgeous. A pile of the Paul's Scarlet lay at the foot of a ladder. The ladder was propped against the house and led to a window on the second floor, where more of the blossoms sat on the sill.

When he hopped through her window, Briallen had been writing in her journal, but she put down her pen and stared at the man, as she was still prone to doing when she saw something she never saw before. His hair was black, his eyes dark, and he stood in the midst of her room, thin and wiry. He held his basket of blossoms on one arm, staring back at her. Rhiannon, he said his name was, but Briallen laughed. She said Rhiannon was a girl's name. He blushed. He said that he liked the name, and he would use it while he was in Wales.

Briallen eventually stopped asking him where he was from, for it seemed he was from everywhere, every corner of the world, and she relished in the fact that she could not discern it. They spent that spring together, wandering in their grove of elms, traveling out to the Aeron Valley, or down the coast. He told her tales of where he had gone, things he had seen, and his stories seemed to have come right out of her journal. He had sailed the seas to other continents, he told her, and wandered both the barren deserts and the white lands of snow to the far north. She always took his stories as truth. He left after that spring, and Briallen spent the long months after looking out her window, and she could not even write in her journal.

When he returned the next spring, lightly stepping from her sill, she told him not to leave her again, and that she would go with him when he once again left Aberaeron. They traveled that year to the places he had told her about. In the winter, while sailing in the

15

Pacific, Rhiannon gave Briallen a ring of jade, and he kissed her full upon the lips. By the following spring, after Briallen had turned twenty, they returned to Aberaeron, and she returned to her dusty home. He left her again soon after, his dark eyes sad as he stepped through her window. Her Aunt Alis moved in with her that summer, as Briallen was pregnant with child, and when she bore a daughter that September, she named it Rhiannon Alis Davies, a proper name for her lovely newborn girl. Little Rhiannon Alis would never know her father.

For the generations to come, Briallen's ring was passed down, given to sons or daughters when they reached eighteen, along with some of her few possessions. Some children would be like her, fair-haired and strong, while others would be born thin, with jet black hair, always causing a relative here and there to raise an eyebrow.

It came one day that Briallen's great-great-granddaughter, Anne, and her husband, Thomas Gillett, had a baby boy, who came to be both fair-haired, like Briallen, but thin and of good constitution, like his forgotten great-great-great-grandfather. He was named Amos, and it wouldn't be long before he started to travel himself.

Chapter 3

New and Old Acquaintances

JAMES HAD A DREAM as he slept in room 103 of the Good
Nite Motel. He was walking in a hazy place, a valley filled with a
blue fog that was sweet to the taste. It lulled one, in this dream-
place, to want to sleep. He wanted to close his eyes while walking
through this valley of silence. But he knew if he did, he would wake
and not discover what was past the curtains of blue haze. So he
trudged on, and his feet sank into the ground with each step.
Farther and farther he walked, until the sludge of the valley was up
to his knees.

Soon, he was walking uphill. The sludge was now up to his hips,
but he waded forward as it flowed against him. As he hiked higher,
the fog began to clear, and by the time the ground was level again,
he could see ahead for some distance. He was standing in a shallow
sea that now came up his chest. The sea was not of water, but of
thick black oil. Ahead of him, a patch of fog started to fade away,
and he could see two figures upon an island. One was a hulking
thing, hairy and nearly eight feet tall. The other was a small figure, a
woman, in a white dress, her wet hair matted around her face and
neck. The beast turned around. It was the Minotaur, and it wielded
an axe in one gigantic hand. Then, the woman turned around, and
James saw a face unchanged from his memories of long ago. It was

his mother, not a day older than forty-three, just as he had last seen her. She had chains on her wrists, and his eyes widened as the Minotaur lifted the axe. He leapt forward, but the fog fell around him again. Its sweet smell overwhelmed him. He couldn't help but close his eyes, and his vision went black.

"Mr. James Henry Worth."

"Mr. Worth, wake up, it's past noon!"

He opened his eyes, and once again, he looked up at black-rimmed glasses, and a small blond mustache. His motel room was slightly lit, only a dull yellow hue coming in from a small crack in the curtains.

The man from yesterday was sitting on the edge of his bed, dressed in a dark tweed suit.

"Good morning," he said. "I'm sure you're feeling much better than you have in a long time, aye?"

He reached down to the floor and lifted a brown leather bag onto the bed. It looked like the bag he had carried with him yesterday, when he freed James from his chains. Reaching inside, the man pulled out a jar, filled with a fluid that looked like molasses. He unscrewed the aluminum lid and offered it to James.

"Do you think you can handle this yourself?" he asked. "It's supposed to help."

James stared lazily at the open jar. Trying to move his arms, he found that he could lift them off the bed, but only about three inches.

"Okay, I see. I guess I'll have to help you out there."

He propped several pillows below James's head and brought the jar up to his mouth. James hesitated for a moment, keeping his lips closed.

"Well, come on," the man said. "I promise you, this will only be good for you. I didn't go through all this trouble bringing you here just to poison you. Just drink as much as you can. Feel it warm up your inside, and then bob's your uncle."

James opened his mouth slightly. The man placed the edge of the jar over James's bottom lip and poured a good amount of the brown syrup down his throat. James nearly choked, and the syrup backed up at his throat. He managed to open his throat and let the syrup flow down his esophagus. Within a few seconds, he felt the warmth spread down his throat and into his belly, and from there, it spread and absorbed into his muscles and bones. All his muscles, every fiber, suddenly tensed, and James nearly screamed as his body stiffened. But soon it stopped, and he relaxed again.

James slowly brought his right arm off the bed. He was able to completely raise his hand above his face. He lifted his left leg up and bent his knee. He couldn't help but wave his arms and legs a bit on the bed, as if he was making little snow angels. He groaned and stretched suddenly, punching a hole in the headboard with his right fist.

"Seems like your vocal chords are working again," said the man. "Well, say something."

James looked at the man but could think of nothing to say. He opened his mouth, but then turned away to the other side of the room.

The man, unflustered, shuffled around to the other side of the bed.

"My name is Amos," he said, slowly. "Some of my acquaintances call me Amos the Quick." He smiled broadly and put out his right hand. It hovered over James. Amos stood there patiently, ever smiling, his hand offered. "Amos, Amos the Quick," he repeated, just in case. His smile was a bit plastic, but not uneasy.

An old instinct gradually fluttered in James's hand. He mechanically lifted it, his fingers dry and crusted like deadwood.

"Ja-," his throat tensed. He squeezed out the next syllables like a cat coughing up a fur ball: "Ja-ames Hen … ry." He was drenched in his own sweat at the effort.

Amos stepped forward and clasped James's hand, shaking it vigorously.

"Aha! For goodness sake, the man's alive. You did it. I did it. We did it! Do you mind if I call you Jimmy? Or Hank? How about J.H.?"

James only stared at him in return.

"Alright then, Jimmy. Today is Tuesday, June 17, 2003. And we are going to get you out of this parched land."

James's eyes glazed over. His mind twitched. He tried to calculate the years that had disappeared.

"Yes," Amos continued, "I was told you've been imprisoned for about forty years." Without any further response from James, Amos straightened up and sighed. He put the lid back on the jar and packed it in his bag. Then he left the room.

It was a few hours later when James slid off the bed and walked into the bathroom. Turning the light on, he stood in front of the mirror. It was a big mirror that took up the entire wall above the sink. When he had hit the light switch, there was no popping sound coming from the wall like he was used to back home. The light was white, illuminating the room instantaneously. He could see the freckles on his dark tanned face. Even hunched over, he towered over the counter in the small bathroom. His long arms hung uselessly. He was broad-shouldered, but the many years of immobility had sapped him of muscle.

The counter was a light beige color, the walls a similar cream color. The sink, toilet, and bathtub were all gleaming white. Crisp, white towels folded neatly hung from shiny chrome racks.

He reached out and brushed the surface of the counter. It was some sort of synthetic material foreign to him. The surface was smooth but with subtle grooves that gave it a slight stone-like appearance. He knelt to the floor and placed his cheek on the counter. It was cool to the touch. He looked at the tiled floor. With a finger, he traced the grooves between the tiles.

He slumped back against the bathtub and thought back to his old bathroom at home. At first, he couldn't remember all the details, but they slowly came back to him. There was only the single bathroom in the house. The first thing he recalled was the colors. Pink and green. The sink was pink, he was sure of that. The bathtub, he thought that was pink also. So was the toilet. Green tiling covered the bottom half of the walls, and wallpapering with a floral design spanned the upper half. A small mirror with a chrome frame hung over the sink.

An uncle named Hugar had paid for the bathroom to be remodeled for his mother's birthday. His uncle had always been offering to pay for things on birthdays or holidays. His mother had picked out the colors and designs—the green floral designs on the walls, the chrome touches, and pink everywhere. James had said he didn't care about the colors when his mother had asked his opinion. But he later wished he had said something, because his friends discovered the new pink bathroom and spent months feasting on the subject. Some of them bought him a football helmet, but painted it all pink with the words *The Pink Express* on it. Somebody also painted his football cleats pink.

These were memories he hadn't thought about for decades. He had been seventeen when last free. Now he was fifty-seven years old. In the mirror, he saw a man still in his twenties. He brought his hand up to his beard. He had never had facial hair. Now the crusted growth spanned from ear to ear, and hair overran his neck and cheeks.

James knew even before his imprisonment that something was not normal. His mother no longer worked, aside from doing some tutoring for the children of friends and neighbors, but they weren't poor. Their house in Goleta was small but custom built, with two stories, right off the beach. They had wealthy relatives, such as his uncle Hugar, who would drop by every so often with lavish gifts. His mother kept their life relatively quiet and normal—he went to the local public schools—and told him nothing about his father.

He was also aware of his extraordinary strength. When he was twelve, he broke the arm of his mother's friend, Morton Hastings, a coach at a high school in town, while play wrestling. His mother spent hours that evening tearfully pleading with James to control himself, and to never exert himself against others. Even so, he was a terror as a freshman in high school, when he joined the football team for a brief stint. The other players, after just one full contact scrimmage, refused to play against him in practice. During two games with the team, he scored fourteen touchdowns, nearly every time he touched the ball as the team's halfback. The feats brought a tremendous amount of attention throughout the town, and once the newspapers started knocking on their door, he quit the team at his mother's insistence.

Nevertheless, he was in no manner prepared for the Minotaur's arrival in his backyard. It was only the second thing he had ever feared up to that point in his brief life. The first was his mother's crying. She was for the most part a lively woman who was strong and courageous. But whenever James did something wrong, her tears would flow, and they wouldn't stop until he felt as guilty as a dog that had been caught peeing on the carpet.

Forty years. A chance existed that she was still alive. She would be eighty-three years old.

He stood up and examined the white, sterile bathroom around him. He turned off the bright lights and left.

Amos was lying on the bed, his hands behind his head, gazing up at the ceiling.

"Oh, hello again," Amos said. "Are you ready?"

James nodded.

"Well, I can see by your non-stop questions that you're a curious cat," Amos said, getting up. "I don't know much, but I'll tell you what I can on our drive back."

Amos pulled out from his handy bag a pair of jeans and a gray T-shirt, handing both items to James. Holding the clothing in his hands, James became conscious of his appearance. His shirt had long ago disintegrated. Only a few threads of fabric were mud-caked into the skin around his neck and chest. His pants had deteriorated into rags, dark with dirt and blood, and no amount of analyzing could tell him which pair of pants they used to be, all those years ago.

He took the faded jeans and went to change in the bathroom. He came out looking uncomfortable. The jeans were tight around his thighs, and then billowed out, leaving plenty of room around his sun-chafed ankles. They were frayed at the bottom and around the waist. He poked at one of the holes along the pant legs.

"That's the style," Amos offered. He tilted his head left and right, and then whispered to himself, "I believe they are, at least."

James picked up the T-shirt and was about to put it on.

"Actually, I highly suggest that you take a shower first," said Amos. "To tell you the truth, you've got quite a scent after all these years in the desert."

James pretended not to hear him and put the shirt on.

"Shall it be windows all the way down in the car, then? Right."

Without anything else to pack, the two were checked out of the motel within a few minutes, and once again, Amos drove his little red car onto the 15 southbound.

Amos had said that he'd tell James what he knew, but that meant everything he knew about himself. He recounted to his mute passenger the story of his coming to America. He had lived in London with his parents through his childhood and adolescent years, leading a life quite mortal. Aside from the fact that he never came down with the cold or flu, Amos was a fairly regular Londoner. He was an above-average athlete—"I certainly think I could have played professional football"—and had plans to join a football club—"once again, it's properly called 'football,' not 'soccer,' you use your foot in football is the first clue."

On his eighteenth birthday, his parents gave him gifts that would change all his plans. His mother, Anne Gillett, gave him a jade ring, passed down through four generations, and along with it, a journal that belonged to his great-great-great-grandmother, Briallen Davies. In the journal, he read of Ms. Davies's adventures when she was nineteen, traveling the world with the enigmatic

Rhiannon. Ms. Davies had written: "He was the God of the Horizon. He was the personification of the longing inside everyone to see what was beyond the next hill, through the next grove, and across the next sea." Most of his family before him had taken the term "God" loosely, attributing it to Briallen Davies's liberty with the language, and a hyperbolic endorsement of a man she fell in love with too quickly. But young Amos had taken it literally. Suddenly, being a football player was too minor—a trivial pursuit. As a lad only four generations removed from the "God of the Horizon," he owed it to himself, and to his family heritage, to seek what was beyond the sea, or at the very least, outside of London. His father, Thomas Gillett, gifted him, naturally, with a leather traveling bag. "This bag has proven useful beyond words, ha-ha." Amos told of his huge ambitions, his grand trip that led finally to the last horizon, New York City harbor. There, looking out the window of the Boeing 747, he saw—

"Jimmy?" Amos asked. His passenger was immensely focused on something outside the car.

James was staring at the side mirror. Amos looked in the rearview mirror, but all he could see was the grey pavement, and the yellow and white lines of the road, all amazingly straight, converging towards the horizon behind them. This stretch of road was eerily empty of cars.

"What is it?" he asked.

James rolled down the side window and looked out and back, his brown hair whipped by the wind. He could barely fit his shoulders through the open window, but he craned his neck and studied something in the sky behind them. This something was behind and above them, keeping pace with the car.

Suddenly, the windshield on James's side shattered. Amos yelled, inadvertently pulling the wheel, and nearly ran the car off the side of the road. James was screaming, and he pulled his head back through the window. A large rock had crashed through the windshield and smashed into his left leg. It was the size of a football, a stone covered with the dust of the desert, and now, with James's blood. His leg was cut deeply.

Half the windshield had collapsed into the car, and Amos struggled to see through the cracked glass on his side. "Bloody hell!" he shouted. "Where did that come from?"

James grimaced, lifting the stone and throwing it outside the car. The veins in his neck bulged, but he could handle pain. He leaned out the window again, this time looking straight up. Charlotte, his beloved acquaintance, flew above them. She was circling high above the car. He looked back to search for Zack and nearly lost his head. He pulled back into the car just in time, as Zack swooped low and fast, passing the car in a black blur, his beak a sharp trail of silver.

"Those are the condors!" Amos yelled. "I was told to watch out for them."

James looked at the backseat. The only thing there was the brown leather bag.

"In the side pocket, there should be a slingshot and some stones," Amos said.

Before James could reach for the bag, Charlotte landed on the car hood, right in front of Amos's view. Her red crest bristled, and her long, white claws clung to the edge of the hood. Amos looked into her blood-red eyes, and he stiffened. James reached out through the hole on his side of the windshield, attempting to grab Charlotte by the neck. As soon as he did, Zack crashed into his arm from above, and his silver beak clamped on James's wrist. He would have bitten right through, but James stifled another scream, and, in a flash, punched Zack square in the body, sending the bulky condor hurtling over the front of the hood. The car buckled violently as the bird landed on the road and was caught beneath the car.

Loud honking blared from ahead. A truck was plowing towards them from the other direction. Amos veered to the right, and as the car careened off the road, James grabbed Charlotte by the neck, and pulled her in.

Dust flew as the car hurtled through the cacti, landing with a loud crunch in a sandy ditch. All the while, James gripped the shrieking Charlotte around the neck and fought off her ripping claws. He kicked open the door and leapt out, clutching Charlotte with his large hands and squeezing hard. Her eyes bulged, but then her neck disappeared with a wisp. Her whole body was gone, a white smoke drifting from his hands and blowing away towards the road. The plume of smoke spun violently, a mass of white vapors with streaks of bright red churning within it. It was a distorted shape, a roiling ball with wings one moment and bursting into a four-armed spiral the next. It moved away from James and towards the road with urgency.

At the side of the highway, it convened with another undulating cloud, this one black, like a ball of industrial age charcoal smoke. James watched as both lengthened, the spirals hardened into limbs, and torsos developed from the tornadoes of smoke. Then there stood two, a man and a woman.

James walked forward with his mouth agape. They were his cousins. The boy and girl he had met. They were grown up, but it was unmistakable. His twin cousins had tortured him all these years in the guise of birds.

Charlotte stepped towards James. Zachary was grasping his left arm, and he slowly limped behind her.

"We came for our meal, but you weren't there," Charlotte sneered. "Your time wasn't done yet, little bastard."

Amos stumbled up the incline to stand next to James, his arms tensed as he strung a rock on his slingshot. Charlotte laughed when she saw the weapon.

"So this is Hugar's man?" she asked.

James turned to Amos.

"Yup, he sent me," Amos answered, his eyes fixed on Charlotte and Zachary. His hands shook a bit as he held the sling-shot. "So these—things—have been eating you, James? Like some kind of bloody Prometheus getting his liver lunched upon every day?"

"Prometheus?" asked Zachary. "That invention of Greek fable?"

"No, our tribute is to a much more ... authentic figure," said Charlotte.

"*Azâzêl*," the twins said together.

"He was a pioneer in the *experiencing punishment* department," said Charlotte, smirking. "But also a much more impressive figure than our prisoner here."

"The Greeks stole the story from the Proto-Kartvelians of the Caucasus, who had named their hero Amirani," said Zachary. "Cultures steal the legends of older societies, and give their heroes their own names. Don't they, sister?"

"Did you like our tribute, James?" asked Charlotte. "You're no *Azâzêl*, but it was great fun while it lasted. My idea, of course."

"My idea, sister."

"Shut up, little brother."

"You were born a trifling five minutes before me," snapped Zachary, turning towards his sister. "You were a conniving fascist, even in the womb."

"Not now, brother," Charlotte said. "But isn't it nice to finally chat, James? Instead of all those thousands of silent, awkward meals we've had."

"He's not very chatty, is he?" asked Zachary. "As dumb as he's weak."

"Let's not waste any more time," said Charlotte. "We have appointments." The two siblings began to walk towards James and Amos.

Amos nervously pulled the stone, and then he released the shot. The stone whistled through the air and struck Zachary in the shin. Zachary howled, and black wisps of smoke sprouted from his wound. Whatever Amos had shot from the sling, it was causing Zachary pain.

Charlotte exploded with a blast of air and smoke, and her condor form flew to Zachary. Her claws clamped down on his shoulders, and she began to lift him off the ground. They rose into the sky, and Zachary hung from her claws, his dark eyes fixed on James.

"Come back down here!" Amos yelled. "Have some bottle, will ya!"

The two men could only look up into the blue. Charlotte soared into the sky, and then she and her brother were gone.

Chapter 4

Go West

THEY WERE SITTING in the back of a bus. James thought about his two cousins. He pictured them from all those years ago as young children. He pictured them as condors, eating his flesh. They knew the sapidity of his blood. They were versed in the piquancy of his liver. He knew the ferocity of their long, serrated beaks and was well aware of their gluttonous appetite. He wondered why they hated him so viciously. For the first time in a long time, he remembered the "Lady of Dreams," who claimed to be his father's wife. She was somehow behind all of it. But if she was some sort of witch who conjured such monstrosities, what did that make his father?

Earlier, Amos had decided to leave the little red car in the ditch, and for that, James had been pensive. The car had rescued him from the desert. He had pulled it out of the ditch, grabbing it right on the rear axle and dragging it until it was on the side of the road.

Amos was impressed, saying, "Look at that!" repeatedly, the whole time James was pulling it out. Yet, neither of them could start it. The hood was popped up in the front, steam rising from under it, and the left front tire was bent out of shape from its axle. James could only look at it. His strength at that point would only do more damage to the car. Amos asked him to push the car back into the ditch. "To get them off our tracks," he said, which sounded silly to James, but he did it.

Amos had gotten right up to the side of the road, and he stuck his hand and thumb out, while walking backwards down the side of the highway. "We're hitchhiking," he said.

Half an hour later, they caught a ride down to a town named Victorville, where James devoured two lunches. They had pulled into the parking lot of a nondescript diner. He pointed at the item on the menu he wanted, a cheeseburger and french fries. Amos smiled and watched as James held the burger with both hands and stared at it for a good five minutes before he took his first bite. He squeezed and stroked each and every fry before eating them. Once he was done with this first meal, James stared at the waitress until she came over and then pointed at something else on the menu. She didn't look surprised at all, and ten minutes later, a T-bone steak with hash browns arrived at the table. He grabbed the steak with both hands, like he was still holding a burger, rubbing it with his thumbs and enjoying the texture of oil, ground pepper, and meat. He would shovel scoops of the hash browns into his mouth with a couple of fingers. All the lip-smacking and loud chewing as he devoured the steak brought long stares from the local folks.

From there, they got on the bus to Los Angeles. This stretch of the 15 Interstate didn't change much. A flat landscape, dotted at every highway exit with gas stations and fast food restaurants. Billboards constantly urged them to get off at the next exit to try shepherd's pie at some Pete's or Bill's restaurant, or to get a special price at the next motel. After a while, the bus rode over some mountain passes, came down to the flat lands again, and switched onto a different highway—the 10 West to Los Angeles. Houses began to line the side of the road, often peeking over the concrete wall that continued along endlessly. Homes and other buildings swept to the north and south, as far as the eye could see. The sky looked yellow. As James stared out the window, the buildings passed by in a never-ending stream of drab facades, and the yellow haze persisted. Amos said they were taking the bus all the way to the Santa Monica Pier, at the end of 10, and James hoped the sky over the ocean would be blue when they got there.

After getting past the formidable skyscrapers in the downtown area, the haze in the sky finally started disappearing. James looked at the other side of the freeway and saw the lanes packed with cars. He had never seen so many cars in his life—shiny automobiles of all colors of the rainbows, big cars that looked like elephants, and trucks that looked like ships. They all crawled eastward, barely a foot between some of them. He wondered where they were going, and why they were all headed away from the ocean. It was ominous.

"Just the flow of traffic in the late afternoon," Amos said. "In the morning, it's all going the other way, westward."

James watched the herd of cars going east for a while, imagining each one of them, with its people sitting inside—mothers and fathers, sons and daughters, waiting to get home. He wondered which exits they would take. He had seen so many on the way: Crenshaw, Fremont, Garfield, Rosemead, Azusa, Grand, Garey, Vineyard, and Haven—names that sounded like they belonged to presidents—all the way back to the 15. The houses continued to cover the land out to the horizons. He wondered what brought so many people to this desert land.

When they reached the end of the line, it was the ocean James remembered, and a blue sky, too. All the questions in his mind dissipated once he saw the arch. A great, green arch signaled visitors' arrival to the Santa Monica Pier. "Yacht Harbor," it said in big lettering, then "Sport Fishing," "Boating," and "Cafes" in progressively smaller lettering. Little stars separated the words to brand the significance of the opportunities at hand. Each time his mother brought him down to Los Angeles from Goleta, they would make sure to come and walk underneath the arch and all its promise. They never sport fished, or boated, but they enjoyed the cafes, and the merry-go-round, which the arch did not advertise. The crowds on the pier would be in their casual best. Women wore dresses with a full skirt and tight waist, perhaps with a platter hat on. Men donned white or beige ice-cream suits, proud of their well-greased hair. He looked around now and observed that the pier and the beaches had been taken over by throngs of under-dressed families and couples. The men were not in suits, but rather shorts and T-shirts. An army of shirts were adorned with advertisements for beer, or for what looked like sports teams and music bands, along with the occasional skull.

Women wore shorts, or skirts that stopped above their knees, and down on the beach, they walked around with only strings and patches of cloth. James had never seen so much of a woman, and he was embarrassed. He glanced at Amos, who didn't seem to notice the almost-nude women at all. As he continued to watch, the attire started to make some sense, especially when he saw them wading in the water. Mothers were picking up their small children and walking them out into the timid surf. It was a different world. The city had moved away from modesty and restraint in the past fifty years. *Did this happen day by day? Or was there some sort of revolution?* Amos had been right; James would fit in with his simple T-shirt and his ill-fitting jeans.

At the end of the pier, behind a Mexican restaurant and away from the crowds, James waited, leaning on the old wooden railing and peering into the sea. Amos had gone to make a phone call. It was well past six in the evening, but here in Los Angeles, in the middle of June, the sun was still well over the horizon. Beside him, along the railing, men sat on the pier next to their buckets and fished.

"You want a churro?" Amos had come back.

James grabbed it. It was gone in three ecstatic bites, a lining of cinnamon on his lips the only evidence of the former churro.

"It won't be long now. Hugar is sending out one of his waiters to pick us up."

He shrugged. For the moment, he didn't care. He could stay on that pier for the next year if need be. If only he could get a fishing rod for himself, he would catch fish every day from the end of the pier. He would build a fire underneath the pier, cook and eat, wade through the water, and sleep each night on the sand. He would watch all the people, with their funny bits of clothing, big sunglasses that covered half their faces, and the strange loud music that they carried with them onto the beach.

"Hugar's at his restaurant in Santa Monica," Amos continued. "Considering the situation, his employees there are the only help he has. And me, of course."

James felt only a tinge of excitement at the possibility of seeing his uncle. Hugar might have some answers; perhaps tell him if his mother was still alive. He might know who the white-haired woman was, or why James was still alive and young, after so many years in the desert. But he also felt dread—a sneaking dread that he was only at the beginning of more trouble. *Things were to be expected of him. But what?* He had nothing to give. Nothing at all.

Amos gestured for them to start moving again. James leaned on the pier railing, looking at the curving coast, the empty blue sky above it. Palm trees swayed in the wind wherever his eyes looked. People were lying on their stomachs and letting the sun paint their skin. Children made crude sculptures out of the wet sand, the waves tickling their feet. He wanted to stay there and forget everything, but Amos kept calling for him. He now had expectations to meet, and it flustered him.

Hugar's waiter was named Quetzal. He picked the two of them up on Ocean Boulevard, right off the pier, in a big, black truck, shinier, and more intimidating, than any truck James had ever seen. The seats were cream-colored, and leather. He could make that front seat his home; it fit him so well. It wasn't so much a truck, as James remembered a truck, as it was a rolling luxury suite. Quetzal was a thin, but strong-looking man. His skin was a natural bronze, and his hair was black and slightly curly. His arms were wiry, his hands firm on the steering wheel. Though he looked young, perhaps in his early thirties, his eyes had a deep, aged quality, as if he'd traveled to the ends of the world and back and seen every turn along the way. He had a wide grin, and he talked at ease the moment the other two men put on their seatbelts. James was comfortable, because Quetzal took the pressure off of talking. He envied this ability to ride the surf of dialogue, never lacking for thoughts, words just tumbling from one's tongue.

Quetzal drove along the streets, declining to get back on the freeway, as the traffic going east was still unappetizing and instead headed eastward on Broadway. He turned southward on Lincoln and eastward again on Pico.

Quetzal said he was named after the awesome god, Quetzalcoatl, the ruler of ancient Mexico who was praised endlessly in the days of Tula. His namesake was "the great plumed serpent," he said. He told the story of Quetzalcoatl's rule over the Toltecs, his struggles with the evil Texcatlipoca, and his trek east and conquest of the Maya of the Yucatan, who called him Kulkulcan. He weaved these tales as the truck cruised smoothly along the handsome grey roads, and he continued at the many stops made at innumerable traffic lights. James and Amos were both quiet, tired from their day on the road, and Quetzal understood this.

After a short while, he turned down a small street and then parked behind a small restaurant. He didn't move to exit the truck, though, turning instead in his seat to Amos and James.

"One day, Superman was flying in the sky," he said. "You know, he was doing his superhero thing, checking out for bad guys, surveying the land. Do you guys know this one?"

James and Amos both shook their heads.

Quetzal began to animatedly tell a joke involving Superman, Wonder Woman, and the Invisible Man. The bawdy tale bore no high respect for any of the three superheroes. He finished his joke, grinned, and with that, he turned off the engine and got out of the truck. James had never heard that joke before. He didn't laugh out loud, but he was a bit tickled inside his stomach. Amos, sitting beside him, found it repulsive.

James glanced over at Amos, who said, "Superman would never do that."

So, the three of them went through the back door of the little brick building on that corner, and through the kitchen.

"Please wait in here, fellas," Quetzal said, pointing them into a small office by the kitchen.

Chapter 5

Hello, Uncle

THE TWO OF THEM sat down in two chairs, facing what must have been Uncle Hugar's desk, a simple wooden thing that was clean, with no papers piled on top. Some kind of gray box sat on the desk. On top of that box was another contraption. Both objects had multiple cables connected to the backside. James leaned forward and easily lifted the top item. He turned it in his hands. On the opposite side was what looked like a television screen, but the object was small and thin, lighter than any television set he had ever seen.

"You have to touch everything, don't you?" asked Amos.

"That's a computer monitor," came a voice from behind them.

James looked back, and then he gently put the monitor down. Uncle Hugar stood in the doorframe of the office. He wore a black blazer over a white T-shirt and gaudy pants with a print that zigzagged in browns, reds, and oranges. His head was full of thick gray hair, and a trim, peppered beard surrounded his wide grin. James searched his own eroding memory of his uncle. Beside the colorful attire, the man looked much like he did back in 1960, if he could trust his recollection.

"Sir!" Amos said, shooting up from his chair.

"Unc-," James stammered. The word stopped, unfinished, in his throat.

"Well, finally, you're free." The older man edged around James's chair and embraced him.

A memory came flushing into James's mind, of a bear hug similar to this one. James was surprised to find himself suddenly sobbing. His shoulders softly convulsed. Hugar strained to hold him up. Amos leaned back against the wall. He didn't want to interrupt the moment, but he was embarrassed for James, who didn't act the way he expected him to act. After a few more moments, James regained the strength in his legs, and he straightened up.

"You look alright, my boy," said Hugar, as he clasped James on both shoulders. "After all these years, you're not only alive, but I see some strength yet in you. My, my." He looked over at Amos. "Mr. Gillett, my good man, wonderful job. Splendidly done!"

"Oh, it was nothing, sir," responded Amos. "Your directions were spot-on. I just had to apply a little of my agility, my resourcefulness, my intellect at the appropriate moments—for example, such as when those nasty birds showed up."

"Zachary and Charlotte? You faced them?"

"Yes, we did, as a matter of fact. But your fabulous sling-shot, along with my superb aim, made quick work of them, and they flew off."

"Yes, yes, thank you once again, Mr. Gillett. You deserve the highest commendation."

"No mention, sir, absolutely no mention!"

"As promised, Mr. Gillett, I am pouring my full attention into your personal matter. I have the utmost confidence there will be a breakthrough very, very soon."

"Oh, that is wonderful, sir!"

"Mr. Gillett, listen here. Mr. Montero has had some car trouble tonight. Unfortunately, we don't have his services for the dinner shift today."

"Oh, yes, okay. So you're lacking a busboy tonight."

"That's right."

"Exactly, right, so I'll be the busboy, tonight. Again."

"And it is so absolutely appreciated, Mr. Gillett. If you don't mind, of course."

"No, sir. Not at all. With all honor, I am at your service."

"Marvelous. Thank you, once again, Mr. Gillett."

Amos left the office, and James faced his uncle alone. Hugar sat down in a chair. He looked at James, keeping the smile on his face, but tears were forming in his eyes. Hugar's face grew red, and soon the tears flowed down his cheeks.

"I'm sorry, my boy," Hugar said, wiping his tears away with his jacket sleeve. "It's been some lonely years, mighty lonely years. I didn't know how I would feel if I saw you. I didn't know if we'd really find you, to tell you the truth. But I had some good intelligence, some damn good intelligence. And here you are."

James sat down and remained silent.

"It's going to be okay, now," Hugar said. "Everything is going to start coming together. I wouldn't worry too much about Zachary and Charlotte for the moment. I have an, er, asset, who is keeping a close eye on them. At the moment, they're not in California. You will be safe here with us, my boy!"

Hugar let out a big sigh. It seemed years of tension were released from his body. He smiled at James. "But you! You must have some questions for me."

Questions. James had hundreds of questions but could voice none of them. He looked down at his hands. He looked around the office. A picture frame hung on the wall. He stood up and walked over to it.

The photo hit him like a lightning bolt. The black and white photo was old, wrinkled, and yellowed. Hugar was in the photo, wearing a suit and holding a hat. His hair was shorter, but he still had the same white and gray beard. James was behind his uncle, lying in the hammock in the backyard of their house. It looked like he was about twelve at the time. And there stood his mother. She wore a turtleneck and capri pants. Her black hair was tied up in a French twist, with her bangs falling down and covering her forehead. James remembered—this was her Audrey Hepburn phase. His mother's smile shone even more brightly than Hugar's toothy grin.

"Mom," James said.

"Yes, lovely Emilia."

"Ques— … questions," James said with some difficulty. He took the picture frame in his hands and stared at the photo.

Hugar walked over and gently pried the frame from James's hands. He unlatched the back of the frame and brought the photo out.

"Here, take care of it," he said, giving the photo to James. "It's yours now." He hesitated before continuing. "I don't know if she's alive. But, I certainly want to hope that there's a chance."

James felt dizzy. Clutching the photo in his hand, he fell backwards, against the wall. Then, he slumped to the ground. He pulled his legs in, put his arms on his knees, and dropped his head. His breathing became shallow.

"I'm sorry, James," said Hugar. "This is all too much at once. All too much."

Hugar shuffled away, and soon he was back with several other people. They took James by the arms and lifted him up. Men were talking, but their voices sounded muffled. The men grunted as they dragged him out and put him in a car. He lay on leather seats. It smelled like the black truck. Then, he lost consciousness.

When he woke, it was dark. He could make out white walls around him. He was lying on a bed, on top of the comforter, like his first night of freedom in Barstow. He looked over at the bedside table and saw "3:08 AM" in ominous red digits and letters. The zero and eight looked like red demon eyes and a mouth. The eyes glared at him from the dark, and he stared back until he fell asleep again.

He opened his eyes. He didn't know where he was. A ceiling fan hung above him. A little light splashed thin white lines on the ceiling. He looked to the left. Window shutters were drawn, but he could see daylight outside. *Nothing to see. Nothing to see.* He slept.

It was dark in the room again. He wondered how long he had slept. *A day? Two?* He turned his head to look at the clock with the demon eyes. A piece of paper was stuck on the front of the clock, partially obstructing the time. It had writing on it. He wanted to reach out with his arm. He wanted to but couldn't. He decided to give up and sleep.

He was awake, but he kept his eyes closed. Whispers fell around him.

"… days now. How long are you going to let him sleep?"

"Do you think he's in a …"

James faded back into sleep. In his dream, he was in his hammock. It was summer. His mother was in the house entertaining guests. He could hear parts of their conversation floating out the kitchen window.

"… wonderful hairdo, Emilia. You look just like Audrey Hepburn."

James stretched out in his hammock, and he slept the summer night away.

Chapter 6

To Wake Another Day

H E SAT UP. Light flooded the room. Someone had pulled open the window shutters. His head felt like an anchor hanging from his neck. He rubbed his eyes. On the bedside table, small squares of paper were stuck all over the clock. He perused through some of the little notes. "It's been four days, meet us at the restaurant, 9 a.m. tomorrow," said one. "It's been ten days, meet us tomorrow at 9 a.m.," said another. "Get your ass up!" said another in a different handwriting. Another piece of paper had a crude map drawn on it. *Route to restaurant*, he thought. He looked at the clock. The red digits said "6:47 AM."

James walked into the bathroom. On the counter, he found a straight razor and some shaving cream. The razor had a beautiful pearl handle with the initials "H.R." engraved into it. He remembered watching some of the older football players shave with straight razors in the locker room. With some difficulty, he unfolded the silver blade out of the handle. His hands shook as he held it. He put the razor down.

He decided to shower. Stepping into the gleaming bathtub, he fumbled with the various knobs until water finally sprang from the shower head. He didn't know how to adjust the temperature, and the water was cold. He had to stoop and crane his neck to get his head under the spray. When he did, the tub quickly filled with blackened water. Globs of dirt began to wash from his hair and skin. He scratched at thick layers of clotted blood that caked his torso. After some time, he just knelt down in the tub. He let the cold water wash over him until finally it ran clear and clean into the drain.

He left the motel room, following the crude map that had been drawn for him. The neighborhood was all concrete and plaster. Yellow and limp grass grew on the sidewalk. James passed a gas station, video rental store, and a Mexican restaurant. He saw a building with a sign that said "Gentlemen's Club." On the sign was a picture of a young woman in lingerie. She wore shiny lip gloss and leered at James.

He was crossing the street when he heard the flapping of wings. On the asphalt, he caught the shadow of birds flying overhead. He ran forward but tripped on the curb of the sidewalk. His forehead crashed against the concrete. Pain seared his brow, but he quickly turned onto his back and looked to the sky. Nothing was there. He looked back over the intersection and saw two crows settling on the arch from where the traffic lights hung. He eyed them for a few minutes, but they gave him no heed.

He pulled himself up and continued on. As he walked briskly west, and then north, the grass became greener. Palm trees began to line the street. He could smell the ocean. He turned into an alley and soon after found the back of Hugar's restaurant. No cars were there, but the back door was unlocked. He went inside.

It was a little before nine o'clock. No one was there. He sat at a table and waited. The wall clock behind the bar seemed to be a bit fast. He watched the seconds hand swing around the perimeter of the clock, marching diligently past the numbers. It hurried by the *5*. It continued past the *10*. Past the *15*, the *20*, the *25*, the *30*. *How many seconds did I spend in the desert?* He became lightheaded.

The *0* was the undisputed boss, standing over all the others, scrutinizing the clock hands as they went by. Were they moving fast enough? Slow enough? Was each step the right distance? The *55* stood anxiously, waiting at the end of each rotation. *Go faster, you're lagging behind!*

James looked again and saw that it was already a quarter to ten. The walls of the restaurant melted away.

He was suddenly hanging and baking in the sun. The manacles were still digging into his wrists. His wrists were cut and bleeding, but forever healing. The metal sliced into his skin as his body was pulled by gravity toward the ground, but his skin refused to submit, regenerating cells, re-growing itself as an unending response.

Zack and Charlotte appeared, flailing their beaks back and forth, bits of flesh and blood flying under their assault. James went into shock, his consciousness transporting to another place.

He was a football player again, playing an endless game in the desert. He was the quarterback, throwing the ball long in a sandstorm. He was the wide receiver, fighting through triple-teams, quadruple-teams, to catch the ball. He was running free toward the end zone. But there was the Minotaur, waiting for him at the goal line. There was the beast, obliterating him with a tackle. The game went on past four quarters, past eight quarters. It went on for a hundred quarters and remained a scoreless battle, as he continually met the Minotaur at the goal line, continually was obliterated with a tackle.

The sandstorm intensified. Just as quickly, it lifted. He was wearing white.

He was a chef at a gourmet restaurant. All the chairs were upholstered in silk and leather. The plates were fine china, the cutlery sparkling silver. People, impeccably-dressed, filled the restaurant, sipping on lemonade and Kool-Aid drink. The waiters and waitresses rushed around, writing down their orders. His mother, Emilia, sat at a table of gold, encrusted with diamonds. She stood up, raised her glass, and declared, "Give me your special of the week!"

Murmurs arose around the restaurant hall, and then everyone

cried out, "The same for us! The special of the week!"

James worked frantically in the kitchen, pulling condors from the crates, de-feathering, gutting, and cutting. He sliced and seasoned, stuffing condor after condor. But it wasn't enough, the orders kept pouring in from the guests—"The special of the week, please!"

The scene shattered, and he was awake.

Someone was gently slapping him on the side of the face, saying, "Come on. Snap out of it."

James looked around. He was still in his uncle's restaurant. The seconds hand on the clock was creeping past the 55, approaching the 0. It was almost eleven o'clock.

Quetzal stood over him.

"Sorry, we got a little confused this morning," he said. "Amos thought it was my turn to wait here for you, and I thought it was his turn. I've got to get the restaurant ready, but Amos will come by and show you around town." He smiled. "Welcome back to life."

Amos arrived about fifteen minutes later, his hair still disheveled and his eyes looking like they could barely remain open.

"Pardon me, friend, I was up late last night. You need to watch out for that Quetzal. The man can really hold his tequila."

James began to imagine Quetzal holding a bottle of tequila in his hand, while balancing on one leg. Then, he imagined Quetzal holding a gigantic bottle of tequila that was hanging off the side of a cliff.

"Jimmy, are you coming?" Amos was standing at the door, waiting. "I'm supposed to get you acclimated to the real world. We've got lots to do."

The two of them took the truck and drove a short distance back toward the Santa Monica pier. Amos pulled into a parking structure just a few blocks from the pier. He had to wait patiently, as James was mesmerized by the many rows of cars, trucks, and SUVs. The parking structure catered to the throngs of people who shopped at the nearby 3rd Street Promenade, and the clientele tended to drive glimmering new automobiles from companies such as Mercedes Benz, BMW, or Land Rover. Amos crossed his arms and looked at his watch, as James stopped at every other car, caressing the wax shines and aggravating the car alarms that beeped their warnings.

"It's my job to teach this overgrown boy about the world," he sighed.

On the day's agenda was a shopping tour. Amos needed some new slacks, and he had several of Hugar's credit cards. It was a teaching moment, then, when while purchasing a pair of leather shoes, one of the credit cards was declined.

"Now Jimmy, all you need to know in situations like this is that you can always try the other credit cards. You see, the MasterCard may not work in this case. But here, see, you have a Visa, and an American Express card. In my experience, the American Express should usually work because those balances must be paid off by Mr. Hugar each and every month."

Indeed, the American Express was accepted.

"No worries, milady, you can turn that frown, upside down," Amos said to the cashier woman.

Another valuable opportunity for education was taken by Amos while they were in a clothing store. As they were perusing the neckties, a salesman approached and asked, "May I help you with anything?"

Amos turned to James. "Do you remember what to say in this situation?"

James stared blankly at Amos, not even looking at the salesman.

After a few moments of this, Amos turned to the perplexed salesman and said, "No thank you, sir, we're only looking."

"Remember, 'we're only looking'—that's an important phrase. Salespeople are always coming up to you and bothering you. It's part of their training."

The next morning, Quetzal was waiting in the restaurant by the time James arrived. They took a flight of stairs down into the basement, and James was surprised to find a boxing ring.

"Do you know why they call this a boxing ring," Quetzal asked grimly. "Even though it's undeniably a square?"

James looked at him and shrugged.

Quetzal furrowed his brow, stiffened his jaw, and leaned in towards James.

"I don't know either. I was hoping you could tell me." Quetzal grabbed his belly and laughed. "Ha-ha, *you*, tell *me*!" He wheezed and reached out an arm as if he needed to hold on to something lest he fall to the ground.

James was caught up in the beginnings of a fairy tale of how the boxing ring got its name. Quetzal regained his composure and looked at James.

"Oh, no, you don't. Don't go off into La-La Land again. Stay here with me." He grabbed James by the shoulders and then gestured with his index and middle fingers between their eyes. "Got it? Stay here with me."

James nodded.

"Say it. Say 'got it.' Vocalize, please."

After some hesitation, James said, "Got it."

"Good, good. Now listen. Hugar wants me to train you, okay?"

"Why?" James asked.

"First of all, you just slept for almost two weeks in your motel room," Quetzal said. "We need to get your blood flowing. Second of all, Hugar has plans for you. He can fill you in later, but regardless, you need to protect yourself, don't you? There are some bad people out there, and right now, you need some work. After sitting on your butt for forty years, we need to get your body moving again. You might have some badass potential, but right now you're at level zero, couch potato status."

James shrugged.

"Over the years," Quetzal continued, "I've picked up a few things—a little boxing in Mexico, a little jiujutsu in Brazil. Heck, even a little aikido in Japan. But, don't even think about doing any sparring today. Today, we start at the basics."

Quetzal grabbed a pair of baseball gloves from a bin and gave one to James. He squeezed the old leather. A memory flashed. *Small hands. I'm trying a baseball glove on for the first time. It looks humongous. I like the feeling of a baseball hitting the web of my glove. The thud it makes.*

A baseball bounced off his chest.

"Hey, hey! Stay with me!"

Quetzal had another baseball in his hand. He lobbed it gently at James. A long-buried reflex fluttered in his arm. James brought his gloved hand up. The baseball bounced off the outside of the webbing.

"Here comes another!"

His glove came up and missed the ball completely again. Another ball came and hit James square in the forehead. Quetzal needed a few moments to recover from laughing. Ball came again, and glove came up. Ball bounced off again.

"Open your glove! You can't catch the ball with a closed glove!"

James spread his fingers. He felt a tingling sensation through his left hand. Ever since Amos saved him and had him drink the strange molasses, different parts of his body were waking up and falling asleep at different times—not to mention different parts of his brain.

Thud. The ball hit his glove's webbing.

"Yes! Success. Now throw it back, softly."

James dug into the glove with his right hand. His fingers felt numb, and he fumbled for the ball. It fell to the ground as he tried to get a handle on it. They kept at it for another hour. Around ten-thirty, Hugar and Amos came down to the basement.

Hugar hugged James and gave him a kiss on the forehead.

"How is it going?" he asked Quetzal.

"About what you'd expect. It's almost like he's regressed since Amos fetched him from the desert. Fine motor skills are real rusty."

"Do you think it'll take long to get him ready?"

"Well, I'm no physical therapist, but I can get him in shape again. That just takes time and effort. But it's the mental thing too. You have to keep him focused. He drifts off, barely says anything. Feel like I'm talking to myself the whole time."

"Really?" asked Amos. "Me and him seem to always have some great conversations. Don't we, Jimmy?"

Hugar and Quetzal glanced at each other and smiled.

Meanwhile, James had been staring at the baseball glove. A memory of a baseball game from long ago had resurfaced. He saw throngs and throngs of people. Something electric was in the air. Then, more and more details came flooding back. It was not just any game. *1959*. He and some friends had gone down to Los Angeles. It was Game Three of the World Series, the first Series game to ever be played on the West Coast.

"Ninety thousand! Ninety thousand people here!" his friend had yelled after they snuck into Los Angeles Memorial Coliseum. The Dodgers baseball team had just moved from Brooklyn to Los Angeles the year before. On that beautiful LA autumn day, they beat the Chicago White Sox and drove everyone along the West Coast baseball-crazy.

He caught a foul ball that day. It was a line drive toward left field that hooked foul. James had reached up with his glove, and the ball curved and whistled right at him. He remembered the *thud* when it hit his glove. It wasn't just a memory. It was a dream. A dream come true.

"I love baseball," James said abruptly, looking up from the glove. Hugar, Quetzal, and Amos turned to him.

"That is wonderful, my good boy," Hugar said. "Wonderful indeed."

Chapter 7

Small Conquests

S O THE DAYS ROLLED ON. Five days out of the week, James went to the restaurant to meet either Amos or Quetzal. They were intent on keeping him active. The physical exertion energized James. He felt his body growing stronger by the day. In the mirror, he could see his muscles awakening, filling out his arms and legs. But having to talk and communicate was exhausting. Most days, his mouth felt wired shut, his tongue swollen and useless.

Occasionally, someone else would be there waiting to meet with James. They would ask Tommy, a busboy who worked at the restaurant, to show James around town. Tommy would take the truck and drive him down the coast to Venice Beach, Manhattan Beach, or Redondo Beach. He would stop in Venice Beach and pick up some weed. They would sit on the beach while Tommy smoked.

Each time, he would say, "Hey bro, you're not going to tell the boss about this, are you?" Without a response from James, he would then chuckle and say, "No, I guess not."

Other days, they would drive to where Sunset Boulevard began at the Pacific Ocean, and drive east. They would pass through the clean, wealthy enclaves of the west. The boulevard would curve, rise, and dip past the University of California, past Bel Air and Beverly Hills. They ventured through the gridlock and traffic of

Hollywood, past burger stands, fitness gyms, and garish nightclub venues that loomed on the side of the boulevard like centuries-old palaces. The neighborhoods would deteriorate as they headed east. Buildings became more drab, the cars on the road less shiny, and graffiti more abundant. At some point, Sunset Boulevard ceased to exist, and they would meander through potholed streets until they were cruising past the wholesale warehouses and homeless denizens of downtown Los Angeles.

"Your lesson for today," Tommy would say, "is that you should stay west, young fella. West is where the loot is."

A few times, James would arrive at the restaurant and find a woman named Kate. She was a student at the college down the street and had taped her ad for English tutoring on a light pole outside the restaurant. Hugar had responded and hired her to tutor James. She mostly tutored junior high or high school kids, but tackled her new enigmatic student with the zest and enthusiasm of a Midwesterner.

She had him read passages from *Hamlet*, *The Sun Also Rises*, and *The Catcher in the Rye*, and then insisted that he tell her how the readings made him feel.

"Words are your magic spells," she enthused. "They are your entry tickets to the circus of life."

To Shakespeare, James said, "I don't know."

To Hemingway, he again said, "I don't know."

To Salinger, he said, "Not sure."

And to each answer, Kate's eyes lit up, and she clapped her hands in approval.

Amos, when they met, would usually take James to run errands. Any life lessons, or way stones on James's road to recovery, would take place in the process of accomplishing these menial tasks. One morning, they went to the mall to purchase new cell phones. Amos had insisted to Hugar that everyone needed the newest phones which were capable of sending text messages. Amos prepped James about the process, and had James handle the transaction by himself. This turned out to be a long awkward endeavor, since James knew nothing about concepts ranging from call-waiting and voice mail to "anytime minutes" and two-year contracts.

The cell phones, once finally in their hands, were a marvel of gadgetry.

"Do we plug them into the wall?" asked James.

"Yes, to charge them," Amos answered.

"Charge them?"

"Yes, to recharge the batteries. You know, electrical power."

"And the phone lines?"

"What? Oh I see. Gosh, sometimes I forget who I'm talking to. Actually, they communicate through the air."

"Through the air?"

"Yes, I believe there are satellites in orbit around the earth. These satellites talk to each cell phone and enable the cell phones to talk to each other. Simple, isn't it?"

"No, not simple."

James had no idea what a satellite was, but the little phone was unbelievable technology. He suddenly pictured a man in a spacesuit. The man wore the spacesuit, brandished a stun gun, and had a spaceship. *Captain Comet*. It was his favorite comic book superhero. The phones were the sort of gadgetry he read about in comic books.

"Are there stun guns now?"

"Stun guns?" Amos was busy fidgeting with his new cell phone. "Well, I suppose so. We have something called Tasers. They send electric shocks through you, incapacitate you."

James's eyes grew big and wide. He asked, "Spaceships?"

Amos looked up from his phone. "Jimmy Hank, aren't you talkative today. Spaceships, sure, there are spaceships. Sort of. Your great nation has quite a space program I would say. They sent men to the moon. They have a space shuttle that sends astronauts up into space every now and again. They have assorted space voyagers and what have you that they've sent out to explore the planets and beyond. Sure, we have spaceships."

James was amazed. The future in his childhood imagination had now become the present. The most powerful technology in his world of the 1950s was the atomic bomb. It was unleashed on Japan the year before he was born. It was the power to wipe out entire cities. Had they now harnessed this grave power, and put it into little portable phones? Into stun guns and spaceships?

"But forget about spaceships," Amos said. "Take a look at this!"

Amos handed James one of the cell phones. He then typed something on his own phone's keypad. Amos then looked expectantly at James's phone. A moment later, it beeped.

"Aha! Yes, now that is technology!"

The screen on James's cell phone had lit up. There, the word "hello" appeared.

"Forget your spaceships. This is 2003, this is text messaging!"

James stared at his phone. It had a tiny television screen in it. He didn't understand the fuss about this thing called *text messaging*. But he was mesmerized by the little television in his portable phone. He took a deep breath, breathing in this frightening new world, this new atomic world of stun guns, spaceships, and televisions in little portable phones.

The time with Quetzal was usually more focused, and more physically demanding. They always met down in the basement for two hours before Quetzal would start his shift at the restaurant.

"You've got the goods, man," Quetzal told him after a few weeks. "You're a beast. There's no control yet, and no stamina, but that's what we're here for."

They started doing workouts. In a corner of the basement were a chin-up bar, some medicine balls, dumbbells, barbells, jump ropes, and other exercise equipment. Quetzal had James learn an assortment of simple exercises, such as doing vertical jumps.

"Stop flailing your arms like that when you jump," Quetzal would say. "And focus on keeping your balance more than how high you jump."

He would also have James do chin-ups, which was fairly easy. Strength and power, James already had. Quickness, reaction time, stamina—these other qualities were much degraded after so many years of inactivity. They would sit in chairs and throw the medicine ball back and forth. The medicine ball felt light in James's hands, but throwing it with precision and efficiency was the primary challenge. In his first attempt at throwing the ball, he threw it off mark. Quetzal caught the ball, but it had such force behind it, the ball still hit him over his right eyebrow, opening a bloody gash.

As soon as it opened, the wound started healing. By the time Quetzal grabbed a towel to wipe the blood away, the gash had closed and healed.

"You're like me," James said.

"That's right, James. I'm like you." Quetzal smiled.

They went on. James learned how to throw a few punches, starting with jabs and crosses. Quetzal had him throw jab-cross combinations while holding forty pound dumbbells in each hand. They did abdominal crunches with a Swiss ball. They started to jump rope, although James snapped the rope accidently when it got caught on his foot. They advanced to more complex punching combinations, also with dumbbells. They did sit-ups with the medicine ball, while throwing it back and forth.

It took a full week to teach James this series of exercises. Then Quetzal challenged him to do them as a series, spending fifteen seconds on each exercise before moving onto the next. He could do the entire cycle, rest for a minute, and then do them again, until he was too tired to continue.

After a month of training, Quetzal commented that his physique had already changed.

"You are blessed, man. You're already ripped!"

James was beginning to feel like a new man. He had more energy each day, and when he was doing the exercises, his mind felt clear. It felt clear like it hadn't since his youth.

One Saturday morning, with no lesson scheduled, he got the urge to run. He was standing at the door of his motel room after having just woken up. He was still in pajama pants and a T-shirt with no shoes on, staring at the sky. He realized he was no longer afraid. He didn't care if Zachary and Charlotte dropped out of the clouds.

He just started running. His body demanded it. It demanded movement. He ran barefoot until he reached the beach. He did sprints in the sand until he collapsed after thirty minutes.

The rising Santa Monica sun shone down at him, and he had the suffocating feeling that he was in the Mojave Desert again, the relentless rays beating against his skin. He jumped back up and started running again. He sprinted south toward Venice Beach. He saw swinging rings and jumped up to grab them, swinging from ring to ring like a jungle madman. He grabbed the last ring too harshly and tore it off of its chain.

He continued on past the outdoor muscle gym. He glanced at the cartoonish men pumping iron, their veins bulging like worms underneath their skin. He kept going, passing a snake-charmer balancing on one foot on a bucket. A snake slithered along his shoulders as a few people gathered. He ran past the Skate Dancing plaza, where a man with dreadlocks danced in circles on rollerblades, a boom box blaring reggae music nearby.

As he cruised by the tattoo shops, and the artists plying their wares on the boardwalk, a voice cried out.

"Young god of the desert!"

James looked to his right. A woman who had been sitting on a crate on the side of the boardwalk was standing up. Metal littered her face. Silver piercings were in her eyebrow, nose, lips, and cheeks. Beaded bracelets covered most of her forearms. She reached a hand to him.

"Beware the future, desert god," she wailed. "Come to me, and I will reveal your fortune!"

James turned away from her and continued forward.

He ran until his feet had calloused and became like bronze sculptures. He ran until he was sweat-soaked. He ran until his body felt like coiled steel. He ran, trying to leave the desert far behind him.

As summer began to draw to a close, the training with Quetzal changed focus. They began to spar.

"No more fun and games," Quetzal had said. "This is for real."

They wore protective helmets and gloves, but those barely helped. Quetzal's blows were sharp and precise. He didn't hold back.

"You're going to face worse than me, James. Come on, get up!"

James barely managed to hit Quetzal in those early fights. But if there was anything that Zachary and Charlotte taught him, it was to take pain. Sometimes the gloves would come off, and they would grapple. Quetzal could not overpower the bigger man, but he would use James's power against him. If James lunged at Quetzal, he would step out of the way, grab James, and use momentum to fling him out of the ring. If James threw a lazy punch, Quetzal would deflect it and twist his arm into an agonizing lock. Or, he would slip under a punch, end up behind James, and deliver a sharp chop or kick to the neck or legs.

One day, James finally got the upper hand. He faked a right cross, and as Quetzal leaned to avoid it, James delivered a quick jab with his left hand that stunned the other man. He used his right foot to sweep Quetzal off his feet and then pounced on him, pinning his teacher to the mat with his knees and left hand. His right hand drew back for a final blow.

"Why are you hesitating? Come on!" Quetzal said. He spat and cursed, berating James in all manner of language.

If it was one thing James learned in his lessons with Quetzal, it was to not think too long. He struck him across the chin. Blood flew from his mouth. Quetzal was unconscious, but softly breathing.

"Bravo," someone said.

It was Hugar, standing and watching from the steps of the basement. He smiled broadly. "If you can beat Quetzal, you might just have a chance out there."

Chapter 8

Vegas, Baby

J AMES WOKE UP at eight o'clock. *Good*, he thought. Hugar
had declared that they needed to meet this morning to discuss
"the future." But first, there was something he wanted to do. He
had a few hours. He felt alert. He sensed the forward motion of
time, pulling him along.

James walked into the bathroom. He picked up the straight
razor. Looking at the initials "H.R.," he wondered if the razor
belonged to Hugar. He unfolded the blade and checked its edge. It
was sharp. He held it in his hand, making sure his hand didn't
tremble anymore. He looked in the mirror. His long, brown hair
and his beard hid most of his face.

Applying some cream to his face, he tried for the first time to
shave. The blade had a rounded edge and was finely tempered, but
even so, James cut himself several times. It was a tedious process,
but he scraped away at the beard, revealing more of his face with
every swipe. When he was done, he washed away the remaining
cream. He stood for a while, getting reacquainted with his face. He
still had the smattering of freckles underneath his eyes, and the
long chin his friends loved to tease. But there was now a meanness
in the curl of his upper lip.

He grabbed a pair of scissors and cut away at his knotted hair.

Chunks of hair fell away until he saw the boy he remembered. It was him, James Henry Worth. He looked a little older, and more wary. Content, he got dressed and left.

He arrived at the restaurant and found Hugar and Amos already sitting at a table in the dining area.

"Look what we have here," Hugar said.

"Morning," James said. "I decided to clean up a bit."

The words tumbled out, a little less hindered than in the previous weeks. He did not tire as quickly when he spoke.

"You look young, Jimmy," Amos said.

"Sit down," said Hugar. "Susie's about to bring out some masa pancakes, with poached eggs, chorizo, and chipotle ranchera salsa."

Before he finished saying it, a waitress came out with a platter full of plates. She laid out three plates and small containers of the salsa. He hadn't recognized some of the names of the dishes Hugar announced, but his eyes knew pancakes, eggs, and sausage when he saw them. The masa pancakes were light and fluffy, with a pleasant taste to them, the full-flavored chorizo clashed magnificently with the soft eggs, and the salsa had a spicy richness while seeming to cool his mouth at the same time. With every stroke of his fork, James tasted a different mosaic of flavors, and every combination satisfied. He finished it quickly, and it was the best meal he had ever had.

"The cook's good," James said, looking dejectedly at his empty plate.

"It's Quetzal," Hugar said. "He's in the kitchen today."

"I thought he was a waiter?"

"He's a man of many talents. But this morning, James, I want to talk about this brave new world you've found yourself in."

Amos had his head down as he slowly, but voraciously, shoveled his way through the masa pancakes.

"Okay, Uncle," James said. "I'm ready to hear more."

Hugar leaned back on his chair and clasped his hands together. "That is maybe the first thing, my boy." He tilted his head to the left and then to the right, stretching out his neck. He unbuttoned the top few of buttons of his shirt. "I am not your uncle."

James sat calmly with his hands resting on his lap. He slowly nodded.

Hugar continued, "Your father—he is also my father."

Amos looked up from the last bit of chorizo he was poking. "You two are flippin' brothers?" he asked.

"Half-brothers," said Hugar. "My mother, an honorable lady, passed away a long time ago."

"Exactly how long ago?" asked Amos.

"That's not important," said Hugar. "Mr. Gillett, would you like some dessert?"

"Actually a little bit of apple pie would—"

"Good, good, maybe you can find some in the kitchen," said Hugar. "And see if Quetzal needs any help while you're at it. That's a good man."

Amos shuffled off to the kitchen. James looked at Hugar's face. His hair was gray and wild. His eyes were jet black and held a plethora of memories and images locked away within them. He thought, *if I am nearly sixty years old, how old is Hugar?*

"Our father's name is Honus Roosevelt," Hugar said. "He is a man who has made many, many mistakes. But you and dear Emilia. The two of you should never have been made to pay for our father's mistakes."

"Honus Roosevelt," James said. "H.R. So that razor in my room was his?"

"It was at one time," Hugar said. "I've had it since. As you can see, though, I don't shave often."

"You can have it back. I don't want it."

"I understand that you don't want anything to do with our father," Hugar said, "That is fine. Let's talk about your mother instead. Do you think that she might still be alive?"

"I want to believe it," James answered. "If there's anything I can do, tell me."

"Good," Hugar said, smiling. "I believe it, too. All we need is faith, my boy, and it will lead us into the future. That is why I have concocted a plan to try to find her. I am going to send you and Mr. Gillett on a task. I hope this little quest will bring us closer to Emilia." He turned in his chair toward the kitchen and yelled, "Mr. Gillett!"

Amos came out of the kitchen, drying his hands with a dish towel. He rejoined them at the table.

"Now, let's talk of your trip to Las Vegas," Hugar said.

"Why are we going to Las Vegas?" asked Amos.

"You're going to my father's casino, Malinche's Palace. James, you're going to be impressed with what our father has built."

"Is he there?" James stiffened a bit.

"No, he went into exile. We don't know where he is, actually."

"So, who is running his casino?" Amos asked.

"When Father disappeared, his wife, Margaret, had her niece and nephew take over the operations. She didn't want such a profitable enterprise to just crumble."

"Mar-Margaret," James stammered. "So that is the name of our father's wife."

"Yes," Hugar said.

"And so by niece and nephew," James said, "you mean Zachary and Charlotte."

"Yes, those are the two."

"Your lovely cousins, Jimmy," said Amos.

"Your cousins are the children of Margaret's sister, Helena. Their father is Amargat, known in certain circles as the Blackbyrd."

"Is he one of the gods?" asked Amos, leaning forward in his chair. His voice became high with excitement.

"No, Mr. Gillett. He is not a god. None of us are, although some may fall for the delusion. But he is quite formidable. Fortunately, he's not in the picture at the moment. He's kept to himself most of this past century. Zachary and Charlotte are somewhat estranged from him also. Their mother died during their

60

birth, and Margaret had taken it upon herself to raise them as her own children."

"She said—" James began, before clearing his throat. He was remembering his encounter with Margaret. "She said that ... she was the lady of ...."

"Dreams. Yes. She does like to call herself that, doesn't she? I like to call her what she really is—a petty witch. She's not much different than you or I, James. She has a father who is ... special. She likes to think that she is special herself, but she's not. Although, she—not so much our father—built up his wealth, manipulated those who worked for him, enchanted those who would purchase from him, and multiplied his holdings. She facilitated Father's dreams, but she also deals in nightmares, as you know too well."

"The Minotaur," James muttered. "He's my nightmare."

"Minotaur?" asked Amos, wiping the last remainder of salsa from his plate with a finger.

"We have a name for the Minotaur—Borus," Hugar said. "It is a monstrosity of Margaret's making."

"Borus," James whispered.

"At some point," Hugar continued, "Margaret turned to ancient magic. Corrupted by her lust for power, she accessed magic that should have been left dormant."

"What is this magic?" Amos asked eagerly.

"You've heard of Minotaurs before, in old myth," Hugar said. "In ancient times, they were crafted in the depths of the earth, in dark ceremonies which merged the soul of a human being with that of a bull."

"A human soul with a bull?" James shook his head. "That's terrible."

"They're from Greek myth, right?" exclaimed Amos. "Like Prometheus, who stole fire from the gods and gave it to mankind. As his punishment, he was chained to a rock, and an eagle nibbled on his liver every day. Zachary and Charlotte said that James's punishment was a tribute to Prometheus, and Ami—, well, I don't remember the other guy."

"Amirani," James said. "But they said the real tribute was to someone named *Azâzêl*."

Hugar grimaced at the name.

"So who is this *Azâzêl*, Mr. Hugar?" asked Amos.

"Listen, gentlemen," said Hugar. "You're getting too carried away with all this myth. Greek myth, the legends of the Caucasus, they're all stories."

"Except for *Azâzêl*, right?" asked James. "They said he was authentic."

Hugar eyed James for a moment. He hesitated before answering.

"Maybe yes, maybe no," he finally said. "If you look at these stories, many of them have the same themes and events. If you go back far enough in time, maybe you can find the real figures and events that inspired all these stories. But enough of this, we need to talk about the real things facing us."

"These are real things," said Amos. "You said yourself that Borus is real."

"True. But just hope you never meet it," responded Hugar. "Although, if you do meet Borus, it may be that we were very close to the prize."

"And what is the prize, sir?" asked Amos.

Hugar looked at James. "What is your prize, brother?"

"My mother."

"And what about my prize, sir?" Amos sat straight up, his spine and jaw suddenly rigid.

"Well, as I have said, Mr. Gillett, I'm pouring my full attention into your matter."

"I've been serving you for a good five years now," Amos said.

"Duly noted," Hugar said coldly. His eyes flashed briefly at Amos, and he lost his warm smile for just a moment. "Everything is connected, Mr. Gillett. Everything is connected."

Hugar turned back to James. "As for Zachary and Charlotte, we will need their assistance if we're going to hope to find your mother. That is why you are going to Malinche's Palace. Remember, I told you I had an asset who was keeping a close eye on the twins. He'll help you get to them. We must persuade them to help us, if you know what I mean. One moment, I need to give you something." Hugar got up from the table and went to his office.

"I'll need your help, Amos," James said, "like before."

"Sure," Amos sighed. "Amos the Quick, at your service, once again." He looked down at his plate and said nothing more. James looked at his own empty plate with its traces of salsa and syrup. He lifted the plate to his face and licked the intermingled sauces. The plate was spotless after he was done. Amos looked up and shook his head.

A moment later, Hugar came back, carrying a statue in his hand. He carefully placed it in the middle of the table. "*Pharomachrus mocinno*, of the trogon family," he said. "Resplendent."

It was a statue of a bird, carved out of deep, veined obsidian. The bird was postured as if about to take flight, with a proud crested head, and most distinctively, two very long tails that trailed out six inches from its rear. The faint veins of the obsidian seemed to move and twinkle under the lights of the room.

"Now watch," Hugar said.

He placed both hands around the top of the statue, as if he was cupping or petting the bird's head, and then slowly caressed the smooth stone downwards. When he was done, the statue had changed form. The bird was now standing as if perched on a tree branch, its wings resting upon its sides. It looked so much smaller.

"That's a nice magic trick," Amos said.

"You can keep this on you fairly easily," Hugar said, "until the time is right."

He hid the statue in one hand, bringing it close to his chest. Then, with a quick motion of his arm, he threw the statue across the room. The obsidian statue morphed again, as soon as it was out of his hand, and the bird was in the posture of flight, wings fully extended outwards, its tails running now two feet behind its rear.

For a moment, James saw not obsidian, but rather a beautifully plumed bird, its crested head and its shoulders a bright, shiny green, its chest and underbelly vivid red, and those two magnificent tails, bronze-green, curling behind it.

The trogon flew in an arc around the room, and then it was back in Hugar's hand, a small obsidian statue.

"Truly impressive," said Amos. "But, I still don't see how it will assist us with Zachary and Charlotte."

"Will it defeat them in their condor form?" asked James.

"No, that is not its purpose," answered Hugar. "But gather close and I will tell you." He whispered to them his plot, as if fearing for spies.

They moved along the large corridors of the Los Angeles International Airport. Hugar had sent Amos and James to the airport not too long after breakfast. Tickets had been arranged, and Hugar had given them very specific instructions for once they got into Las Vegas. In addition to everything else, Hugar had given James a Malinche's Palace security uniform as a disguise.

Amos dressed in his own disguise—board shorts, a Quiksilver T-shirt, and a wig of long blond dreadlocks. He also put away his glasses. James didn't really know what the end result looked like, perhaps a college student who squinted too much and desperately needed a shampoo. Amos did all the talking at the airport. At the ticket counter, he flashed James's ID card for him, a card given to them by Hugar.

Amos also directed James through the airport—"Alright, just smile and walk through the metal detector. You have no keys, so that's good. Steady, if anybody asks you any questions, just say 'no.' Stand on the right side if you're going to fanny about."

James was thrilled by the moving walkway they were using. He stood still for a while, enjoying the sensation of being carried toward his destination. *This must be how kings felt.* When he did start walking, the world whizzed by him. It was an exhilarating sense of falling forward.

Once on the plane, the large man found his seat incredibly cramped. He kept his shoulders in and pulled his right arm across his body as to not inadvertently knock the little woman on his right in the head.

"So people fly in these things all the time?" James asked Amos.

"Sure," Amos answered. "I've flown six or seven times myself."

"I didn't expect the plane to be so big. Do they ever crash?"

"Yeah, it happens, but it's still a lot safer than driving."

"Really?"

"Yup."

Despite Amos's reassurance, James studied the emergency procedures diligently.

"So what's Las Vegas like?" he asked later during the flight.

"I've only been there a few times, but I can say, it's very gaudy. Everything is blown up nice and big, and anywhere they can put lights up, they do it. The inside of the casinos are lit up like a Christmas tree, and all you hear is the tinkling of the slot machines. It's impossible to avoid, because you can't even go up to your hotel room without going through the casino floor, and the tinkling seduces you like the sirens of *Sirenum Scopuli* used to do—or still do, I'm not sure."

"So people come to Las Vegas to be seduced?"

"Why yes. That's exactly what they come do to. It's sort of like one of those theme parks. You don't see anything that might look like a regular building or residence. They don't want you thinking of work, or of home. And I'll be damned if I ever saw a clock inside one of these casinos."

"So people just gamble the whole time?"

"Some do, some don't. The advantage is skewed towards the casinos, of course, or they wouldn't make any profit. I met this Chinese man recently. My auto broke down in the middle of the night, and Hugar gave me this chap's number to call for a tow. I called him, and he had been sleeping, but he came out, had his own tow truck that he was making payments on. Nice fellow, about my age, and he nonchalantly told me how he had lost a couple of thousands of dollars in Vegas the previous weekend. That's why he was taking all calls, even in the middle of the night. He said he had a wife and two young kids. So I told him, I thought it was a lot of money to lose. He told me it was not a big deal, that he had probably lost about $15,000 that year."

"How much did he make towing?"

"I think he said about $25,000."

"Only $10,000 left for the family," mumbled James.

"Well, I didn't argue with him. After a while, he was arguing with himself, virtually having a little debate about it alone while I listened. Lots of sighing."

James's first airplane ride would not duly impress him. He expected fancy sounds and breath-taking sensations. But he only heard some loud buzzing, experienced a slight upheaval of his stomach upon lift-off, and some bumpiness upon the landing. The true show was out the window, and James nearly suffocated Amos, who sat in the window seat, to lean over and peek out the blue portal.

The flight didn't take long. After an hour and a half, they were traveling by taxi down Las Vegas Boulevard. James, like any first time visitor to the city, spent the entire ride staring out the window. They passed a sleek black pyramid; a castle in white, red, and blue; and cartoonish skyscrapers jammed together. The majesty of each successive casino grew. Each had different mixtures of elegance and audacity. It culminated a few miles down the boulevard with Malinche's Palace.

Unlike many of the other casinos, Malinche's Palace was not confined to one structure. It easily encompassed two or three times the acreage of any of the other casinos. The front, dominant building was a mesmerizing facade of symmetry and architectural grandeur. On a street of lights, glass, and steel, its all-stone walls surprised the eye. Fifty wide stone steps led up to a rectangular face, composed of thousands of stone tablets. The intricate carvings, seen as a whole, created designs ranging from simple squares and diamonds to peculiar compositions of leaves, flowers, leopards, and human beings in elaborate poses. This stone montage protruded at some points, retreated at others, but all flowed harmonically across the entire face. Beyond this structure rose a tall, cylindrical high-rise, gilded in gold.

"Malinche's Palace," said Amos. "Fashioned after the House of the Governor in Uxmal in the Yucatan. The zenith of Maya architecture. Your father certainly had interesting taste. The entire grounds is based on the Uxmal site. Behind here and to the right is the Nunnery Quadrangle. On the opposite side you'll find the House of Doves. The only modern addition is the gold hotel rising above the main structure."

"I think the gold tower is obnoxious," James said.

"It wouldn't be Vegas if it wasn't."

"Are we on time?"

"Just about. I'll just go in now. If I see Charlotte, I'll make a big stink. You focus on finding the brother."

Amos, squinting all the way, continued up the steps and through the automatic sliding doors of the Palace's entrance, trying to blend in with the many tourists sliding into the air-conditioned interior. He would walk through the casino floor and sit down at a slot machine close to the staff entrance at the rear of the casino.

For a moment, James remained on the steps. He took another look at the casino facade. It most likely paid for the house in Goleta, and the car his mother drove. It was strange to not know the face of his father. After a few moments, he circled around the front structure and entered through the rear of the casino. There were no hassles, as Hugar had given him the appropriate passes and identification, along with the uniform.

He used the service elevator to climb to the top floor, where his father's usurped office suite was situated. Two beefy guards stood in the elevator lobby. James nodded at them as he walked towards the suite's double doors, and trying his best to sound nervous, he said, "They sent for me."

After briefly perusing his identification card, one of the guards opened the door and said, "G'luck."

A young woman and an older man sat behind two counters in the next room. James approached the man.

"Mr. Kensington?"

"Yes, can I help you?" he asked crankily, looking up from a crossword puzzle.

"I was sent for," James responded, slipping an envelope to him.

Kensington picked up the envelope and sliced it open with a long fingernail. He looked inside the envelope, smirked, and whispered, "Hold on a sec." He looked over at the young lady. "Becky, I forgot to tell you that Ms. C wanted you to make sure all the staff notices were up this morning."

"I thought you were goin' to do that," she protested.

"No, I'm supposed to brief Mr. Z this morning, unless you want to do that."

"Uh-uh, no thank you. I'll check on the notices," she said, before leaving.

"Are you the, um, asset?" James asked.

"Asset?" Kensington snorted. "Honus sent you, right?"

"Don't you mean—"

"Never mind. Just go inside, kid. The doors are thick—soundproof."

James headed towards the next set of double doors, made of mahogany and carved with a pair of *H*'s. He turned the knob, and walked through. It was a large room, with plush purple carpeting, a pair of black leather sofas, and two large wooden desks, varnished to the color of red grapes. In the corner, glass went from ceiling to floor.

Zachary was crouched on a credenza against the glass wall, haunches low, his knees up by his shoulders. He was staring out the window. He didn't move, and his face was pressed against the glass.

James closed the door behind him, and the sound stirred his cousin.

"Charlotte?" Zachary asked. He looked back, his neck twisting grotesquely. "You!"

Before he finished his utterance, Zachary had leapt off the credenza and over a desk. James was ready, or so he thought. Zachary was lunging over the desk, about ten feet away, but as James's arms tensed—he was going to unleash an uppercut—he found Zachary's hands were already around his neck. James stood at least half a foot taller, but Zachary pulled him forward and downward, and then pelted him with kicks to the abdomen. This all happened within a couple of seconds. James finally unleashed the uppercut he had intended to earlier. He connected, and his cousin flew back over the desk, disappearing behind it.

James dashed forward and jumped on the desk. He looked over, but no one was there. Something struck him behind the knee, and he fell on the top of the desk. Zachary was soon on top of him, hitting him on the neck and in his sides.

James managed to reach back and grab Zachary's shirt. Grunting, he tossed Zachary across the room, bouncing him off the far wall. James pulled a slingshot from a jacket pocket and quickly aimed it at his adversary. He shot and missed. Zachary had vanished into smoke again. The vapors of his being remained floating near the wall. James reached into another deep pocket, and he pulled out the obsidian statue.

The trogon was frozen in its passive pose, but James flung it across the room. It took flight. The vibrant green and red bird streaked through the air, and as it whipped across the room, its beak opened. It sucked all that had been Zachary into its belly. A second later, the obsidian statue once again rested in James's hand.

He was standing on the desk, and the great doors to the office swung open, revealing Charlotte in its frame. She was breathing hard, dressed in a maroon suit. Her hair was a bright red.

Charlotte said nothing and remained where she stood. She

looked at James, and then her eyes searched the room, gazing at one desk, then back at him. Her gaze lowered and rested on the statue in his hand. Her eyes narrowed, then slowly, they widened. James looked down, and he saw that through the dark, opaque stone of the statue, a faint light ebbed.

"What have you done!" Charlotte shrieked. She screamed and ran at James.

He braced himself for her attack, but she crumbled at his feet, her fingers rigid on the statue. She kept screaming, a blood-churning cry that pierced through the rooms and hallways of the entire floor. She then bared her large, shiny white teeth, and prepared to bite his hand. James hesitated slightly, but then struck her across the cheek.

"Payback," he said breathlessly, although he became nauseated for hitting her.

Charlotte groaned and writhed on the ground. Still clutching the statue, James ran from the room. Behind his counter, Kensington lay motionless on the floor, but he opened his eyes as James passed and winked. The two guards in the elevator lobby confronted him, but he ran right through them, sending them careening off his shoulders. He went into the stairwell, leaping down steps upon steps, and he was twenty floors down when he heard Charlotte's screams coming from above.

Minutes later, he crashed through the first floor door. James turned left, then right, searching his mind for an image of the blueprints Hugar had shown him. A commotion came from the left. A group of men turned around a corner. Three guards were dragging Amos down the hallway, heading his way.

James walked swiftly towards the group.

He struck the first guard on the left with an elbow, and then swung to the right with a wide hook that grazed another guard's chin, sending him sprawling to the floor. The third guard turned and ran back around the corner.

More screaming came from down the hallway. Charlotte had

come from the stairwell, and she sat slouched on the floor, pulling at her hair, which looked like flames around her pale face. Her mouth froze open in that never-ending scream.

"What's wrong with her?" Amos asked.

"Don't know," he said. "Let's just go."

Some guilt clutched at him. They rushed down the hallway, and James was glad Amos remembered the lefts and the rights. Not before long, they were out in the harsh desert sun, the thick hot air sending waves of perspiration down James's back as they ran from Malinche's Palace.

A few hours later, when Amos and James were certain that they hadn't been followed, they settled into a small casino off the main strip. They sat at the ten dollar black jack tables, just the two of them and their dealer, Mei.

"I don't know how she did it," Amos was saying. "I pride myself on being attentive, and I was focused, constantly scanning the room. But she appears out of nowhere, taps me on the back, nearly scaring me out of my pants."

"She can do that," James said, paying attention to the two cards in his hands. "She finds people."

He showed Amos his cards, a five of spades and seven of hearts.

"Um, I would normally hit, but the dealer has a five and a ten, so I would hold off, see if she busts," he said.

"But what if the next card is a six? She would get twenty-one. I could use the six, while keeping her from getting it. So why not hit?"

"Because, you'll upset the other players. It could be an eight or something, and you would be the one who messes things up. In these situations, it's best to not have the attention on you."

"But you're the only other player here."

"Well, I would be upset at you."

"Hit me please, Mei."

"Oh piss."

"Six!"

"Well, that's just random luck there. But then I assume you'd have lots of good luck after what you've been through."

"You bet."

"It must be nice though, heh? Knowing your paps is a god."

"He's not a god. And let's not talk about that here."

"Oh, Mei doesn't mind, she must know we're feeling a little squiffy is all. But come on, just give me a taste of what's on your mind, Jimmy."

"I have no interest in my father."

"None?"

"Not at all."

"But why not? Regardless of what Hugar says, your father is some kind of god-like being. Doesn't that blow your mind? Don't you want to learn more about who he is? Who you are? Com'on, he's immortal. He's got power, wisdom—"

"He's got nothin'."

"Well, I don't understand that. I know I'd love to meet my father."

"You don't know your father?"

"Well, I do know my mortal father, yes. Thomas Gillett of London, schoolteacher in the Central London School District. Married to Anne Gillett, who remarkably has never left England. You know, at the age of sixty, my mum still looks like she's forty. Now, I love my father, but my mom could have done a lot better. My great-great-great-grandfather was the 'God of the Horizon.' How could you just end up settling and staying in one place with that kind of pedigree?"

"Maybe she didn't want anything more. Maybe she just wanted your father. Maybe she just wanted you."

"Well, she could have done a lot more than just sit there and raise me. But anyway, the point is, I'll give up anything to meet him. His name was Rhiannon."

"Sounds like a woman's name."

"It is. He adopted it just because he liked the sound of it. In fact, my great-great-great-grandmother, Briallen Davies, wrote that he was called different things in different places he went to. And she decided to name their daughter Rhiannon also, in honor of him after he disappeared. Rhiannon Alis Davies. Half normal, half special—just like you."

"It doesn't sound like these gods make very good fathers."

"Oh quit it."

James grew silent.

They sat there at that table until well into the night, good fortune allowing them to play on the meager allowance Hugar had given them. The casino was more than willing to let them sit and play as long as they wanted. The dealers who came, went, and listened to them chatter about "gods" gave nary a hint that what they heard was anything out of the ordinary. It was Las Vegas, and every mortal, or immortal, was worth as much as the chips in his pocket.

They left their hotel in the morning, after about four hours of sleep. James had a hard time getting up, even as Amos pounded on his door. He wondered why there was such a thing as checkout before noon. They took a taxi back to the airport, rolling past the garish casinos in reverse of the previous day.

A strange sight greeted them as they exited the taxi. Charlotte, her red hair now the color of dry leaves in the autumn, dark eyes looking bruised in the midst of her pale skin, shuffled up to the two of them, hands forward like a beggar in the street.

"Please, sir," she muttered. "My brother, give me my brother."

Charlotte gripped weakly at James's shirt, ignoring Amos completely.

"Hey, do something, brush her aside," Amos said. "She's liable to stab you in the tummy."

She had been looking up pathetically at James, but now her eyes searched about slowly, and it settled on the backpack he had slung over one shoulder. With one hand, she pawed at it.

"It's too evil," she moaned. "Please let him go. I ask you nicely this time. Next time, we won't be polite."

"Get away you!" Amos said, and he shoved her away. Amos looked at a nearby security guard and waved him over, but as soon as he looked back, she was gone.

James was looking up, and Amos saw wisps of smoke floating toward the sky.

"Jimmy, use the statue!"

"No, it's alright Amos," James said. "One is enough."

"She's gone bonkers, she has," said Amos. "Talking in the plural is always a sure sign."

They went inside the airport, away from the intense scrutiny of the Nevada sun. Soon, they crossed over to California, high in the pale blue sky.

Chapter 9

Distant Shores

H E HAPPILY GAVE the obsidian statue to Hugar, once they were back in Santa Monica. James felt there was something eerie about the thing, especially now that Zachary was in it. He had tried to sleep on the plane, with the statue in the backpack right at his feet, but he thought he heard whispers, tiny little wails, calling his name. Amos told Hugar that Charlotte had gone insane, and that she was liable to come and find them. Hugar sent the two of them up north to Santa Barbara, back near Goleta, where he had a little house off the beach, a cozy thin house with two stories and a long rickety wooden stairway down to the beach below.

"Charlotte doesn't know about the restaurant here in Santa Monica," Hugar said. "But she's going to be looking for you now, and we need you far away here. I need some time with the statue."

Hugar was staying in Santa Monica with the statue to see what Zachary would divulge. They hoped that he would be able to give them some information about James's mother.

Amos and James drove a rented car up to Santa Barbara. For a while, James stayed inside of the house, never even venturing down to the beach right below their rear balcony. It was a wonderful house, the first he had been in since he was forced to leave Goleta. The living room had only room enough for a small couch and coffee table. It had no television. The adjoining kitchen was almost as big as the living room, with wallpaper peeling from its brown walls and a creaky blue refrigerator. The water from the faucets of the house took a great deal of time to warm up, and the carpets were worn thin, but James liked it. It felt like a home.

He spent many afternoons sitting on the balcony, enjoying the swaying of the ocean, its love-making with the shore. He watched the gray-blue water break up into a bubbling of white foam, dancing on the sands as long as it could until it was pulled, arms dragging, back into the sea. Some days, the surf would be high, and he thought that nothing embodied passion as closely as the meeting of sea and land, the breaking of waves, the throbbing energy of the aftermath.

He watched as men, women, and children walked along the water, or played just on its lip. The lapping of the waves upon their feet and legs was the sea calling them, urging them to ride its back and see where it played on another shore. One day, Amos came out and sat with him to watch, but Amos's eyes were fixed upon the horizon. He looked not to where sea met land, but where the sea reached for the sky, yet never quite realized its ambition. On this occasion, they spoke.

"I'd like to find her," Amos said.

"Who would you like to find?"

"Rhiannon Alis."

"Why her? I thought you wanted to meet her immortal father, the one who started it all."

"I've fancied that also, but I doubt we'd ever meet. Briallen Davies found him picking flowers in a tree, and I'm not the tree-climbing type. But my great-great-grandmother, she's like you. She is still very much human. She lived a fairly normal life before disappearing across the seas."

"How about your great-grandparents, or your grandparents, they wouldn't be too far removed."

"Yes, that's right. Well, my grandmother, her name was Ceridwyn Gyffes, I did meet her. In fact, until I was seven, we were somewhat close. Besides my mother and I, she refused to see anybody in the family really, and when I was seven, she killed herself, right in Wales where she was born."

"I'm sorry to hear that."

"Yes, it was quite traumatic. Especially since I had the bad habit of calling her me mum also, she looked so young. So young and beautiful."

"It must have been hard."

"Yes, well, Ceridwyn's son, Matthew, had died years earlier. Poor Ceridwyn was losing everyone she cared about. I think she couldn't bear to see any more death in her family, and so she took her own life."

"I'm beginning to think that perhaps my problems are small."

"Well, I wouldn't say my family has had problems. We're just got a bit of longing is all. Matthew, he went over the ocean to look for Rhiannon Alis, you see. Left his wife and my mum, saying he wouldn't be long, just as long as it took to sail to France and back. His ship never made it over the English Channel."

"Nobody knows what happened to Rhiannon Alis?"

"I think Ceridwyn might have had an idea, but she wasn't good for much besides sitting at home after a while. It was such a waste, a beautiful vessel she was, but with no sails on her at all. She hated her own youthfulness, her mother having disappeared, having outlived her husband, and then losing her son."

James looked hard out to the sea as he listened. *So much pain in families*, he thought.

"So now I'll tell you why, Jimmy," Amos said conspiratorially, "why I want to find Rhiannon Alis so much. Before I left England, I hadn't even decided where I would go yet with my new leather bag. I begged my mother for anything she could give me—old photos, belongings of our family that could tell me more of our past. I was quite impassioned about it. Right before I left, she gave me an old letter, crying as she gave it to me. She said it was sent to my great-grandmother Ceridwyn after she had passed away. Well hold on, let me get it.'"

Amos ran back into the house and came back minutes later. He held a yellowed letter with both hands, letting it rest on the tips of his fingers.

Sitting down, he read, "Dear, dear Ceridwyn. I am sorry, for it has been so long. I never wanted to leave you, but I left myself for a long time, and I still struggle to know whom I really am. You have entered into my thoughts again of late, after months of the cloudiness. You know of what I mean, because you wrote of the same feeling a few years ago. I am aware of myself currently, but I fear that this weak assuredness will pass. What I fear more is leaving you alone to the same dread. I am so sorry, my dear Ceridwyn. I struggle to regain myself, and I reach out to you. When I am strong enough, I hope to see you again. Please write to me your condition. I am in America. Perhaps, you will visit me one day? Love R.A."

He put the letter down in his lap. His eyes were bright as he exhaled.

"She was, and may still be, in America," Amos said. "And that's why I am here."

James put his hand on Amos's shoulder. "You will find her, my friend."

"Thanks mate," Amos said. "I was hoping Hugar could help me, but so far, no cigars."

James suddenly felt guilty. Amos had been running all over the deserts of California and Nevada to help find James's mother. Hugar was now busy with Zachary. Amos needed help, but none had been coming.

"Whatever I can do to help," James said. "Just let me know."

Amos smiled. "We'll both find what we're looking for, then."

"That's right."

They sat on that balcony through the afternoon. They shared more with each about family and the pain that comes with it. But mostly, they watched the sea continue its endless work. It came from the horizon, carrying memories from distant lands. It called from the sands which succumbed to its tumult, saying, "Come, come."

Chapter 10

The Daughter of Briallen Davies

RHIANNON ALIS DAVIES was born in 1884 in the town of Aberaeron, just like her mother before her, and many generations of Davies folk before that. Her mother, Briallen Davies, had experienced the most exciting year of her life in 1883—the year she traveled with the man who called himself Rhiannon, the man who would leave her for the last time as she was pregnant with child.

So Rhiannon Alis was thrust into the world, named after a misnamed father and a gracious aunt. Her aunt, Alis, who had never married, tried her best to nurture both her niece and her grandniece. She was father, and she was mother. She was disciplinarian, and she was caregiver. But she was not immortal, and Alis Kendall passed away before Rhiannon Alis had turned nine.

Therefore, Rhiannon Alis by 1893 had experienced two losses— the first being the father she never knew, and the second being her aunt, who had been like an angel. Her mother, Briallen, stuck her chin out and carried on. She worked in a bookstore to support their life in Aberaeron. She would bring scores of books home, hoping that her child would catch the same fire for words and stories that she always had. But Rhiannon Alis mostly ignored pages and books. Since her earliest memory, she had known that the real stories came to her from thin air.

From when she was an infant, cradled against her aunt's bosom, she received stories of boyfriends who were never quite good enough, and of her aunt's battles for independence from the expectations of her parents. These were lullabies that guided her into sleep, told to her without a single voiced word.

By the time she was five, Rhiannon had become aware that the stories came more abundantly when she was in proximity to people. She ventured around her town, sidling up to folks from whom she felt warmth and peace. She discovered that most people worried about things she didn't understand—tasks that they were focused on, or fears that administrated their lives.

She also learned that her mother was often preoccupied with strange stories of foreign places. When she was near her mother, who often was reading at home, she sensed that her mother was gone in a faraway place. Sometimes, late at night when Rhiannon was supposed to be asleep, she would feel sorrow emanating from her mother's room. She would have visions of a man she had never seen before, a man with black hair like herself.

She would ask her mother about the dark-haired man. Briallen would look at her daughter strangely, and Rhiannon would feel her mother withdraw further from her. This was Rhiannon's third loss—the slow loss of her mother.

When she was fifteen, Rhiannon met a boy her age named Owain Morgan. His family had just moved to Aberaeron. Owain was a sensitive boy, and when she was around him, she felt that he would never want to hurt her. Their love affair started swiftly and continued through most of that year, consisting mostly of walking through the woods and holding hands. They didn't talk very much on these walks, but they always knew what the other felt and thought.

When Owain found out that his family was moving again, he cried into Rhiannon's shoulder, and she was wracked by the waves of guilt that emanated from him. It was a grievous guilt, born because he could not keep his own heart's promise to never hurt or abandon her. She tried to speak into his heart to clear him of his guilt, but his own dark voices drowned out hers. On his last day in Aberaeron, she tried to soothe him with her body, the way that her mind and voice could not. In their clumsy way, they consummated a love that was never to be nurtured further.

Weeks after Owain and his family moved away, Rhiannon would find out that she was pregnant. This was her fourth loss, a loss that replicated her mother's. Love had vanished, but it left a new, unexpected life.

Rhiannon now had the same dilemma that her mother had faced. She was left to care for a child in Aberaeron, while the father was somewhere out in the strange, wide world. She watched her mother, quietly coming and going between the house and the bookstore, and reading the rest of her days away in her bedroom. She wondered if that was her future.

She started to notice that the thoughts and stories of the people around her grew darker. Or was it her own thoughts that grew darker? She was not sure. She made a promise to herself that she would raise her child well, and when that child was of age, Rhiannon would leave Aberaeron and not look back.

That child was Ceridwyn, who was born in 1900. With the birth of her grandchild, Rhiannon's mother regained a bit of lust for life. Briallen doted on Ceridwyn, who would grow lush blonde hair and resembled her in both temperament and appearance. Rhiannon drifted further from her family, in mind if not in physical presence. Years later, in 1918, a grown Ceridwyn announced that she was marrying her sweetheart, Govannon Gyffes. Govannon was returning to Aberaeron from his tour of duty at the close of the World War.

Rhiannon put into motion long-simmering plans to leave Aberaeron. Love-stricken Ceridwyn took the announcement in stride. She believed her when Rhiannon said she would return in the near future. In many ways, Ceridwyn and Rhiannon behaved like sisters. Rhiannon still looked like she was twenty years old and exercised little discipline over her daughter. Meanwhile, Briallen, who was then fifty-four years old, acted as mother for both of them, although more so to Ceridwyn.

Briallen did not take Rhiannon's announcement as well. Although she did not say much, Rhiannon knew what her mother felt. The surprisingly venomous thoughts that scorched Rhiannon's mind that day hastened her escape from Aberaeron. Briallen never did forgive Rhiannon's father for his absence, and now the sin was laid upon the daughter. The loss of her mother was now sealed. Briallen would die two years later, never having seen Rhiannon Alis again.

In the summer of 1918, tens of thousands of American soldiers were arriving each week in France. The year before, Germany had provoked the United States into finally entering the war. This had led to the Selective Service Act of 1917, which required all men between the ages of twenty-one and thirty-one to register for military service. In June of 1917, Rainier Rousseau of New York City, whose family originally hailed from Paris, France, happily registered.

He was part of the influx of American soldiers into the battlegrounds of France. By then, Allied forces had begun the Hundred Days Offensive that would catalyze the end of the war. Hostilities wound to an end throughout the autumn, but young Rousseau would linger in the country and reconnect with old family in Paris.

The French countryside was scarred, its population devastated. The French people began an exodus from the farmlands into the cities. As Rousseau discovered the country of his forefathers, people from all around Europe also began to pour into the cities, the greatest of which was Paris. By the beginning of 1919, Paris was filling to the brim with dignitaries and celebrants from around the world, as world leaders from dozens of countries converged in the city for the Paris Peace Conference. Countries would be sliced apart and divided, while politicians struggled over the spoils of war. Paris in 1919 was the center of the universe.

Hope overflowed in the streets, and celebration was the purpose of life. Endless balls, dinners, and other fetes busied counts, countesses, and politicians, while newcomers from the rural lands and beyond tried to assimilate into the new, rejuvenated Paris.

Into the midst of this, Rhiannon Alis Davies arrived and joined the throngs. As she absorbed both the aspirations and phobias of the multitude of people she then encountered, she found herself equally exhilarated, appalled, and overwhelmed.

There was Paris. It looked forward to a new world order. It toasted the high principles extolled by the diplomats of the world. And there was Paris. It hosted a crush of cultures and disparate individuals, many of whom grew insecure under the critical glare of the city. Rhiannon became acutely aware of her lack of stature in this particular society. Judgmental thoughts assailed her attire, and her lack of knowledge of where to place pins, how to wear gloves and veils, or how to properly tilt a hat. She was bombarded.

Both enchanted and repulsed by the city, she questioned whether she had made the right decision to come to the epicenter of the world. But that uncertainty disappeared when she stepped before the bright and wild eyes of Rainier Rousseau.

He had jumped out of an automobile driven by his French uncle. The car had run through a puddle and splashed rainwater on Rhiannon and her already drab dress. In a friendly manner, the American insisted that she come with them and change out of her soaked clothing. Soon, she was trying on the glamorous dresses of Rainier's cousins. Rhiannon blossomed that afternoon as she chatted with Rainier, and his cousins, Lucienne and Emilienne. The girls encouraged her to try on the frocks, satin capes, and silk jerseys in their armoire.

It was Lucienne and Emilienne who befriended Rhiannon and brought her inside of Paris. They took her to lunches to meet friends and began to inculcate her regarding the fabrics, styles, and the various couturier houses that made up French *haute couture*.

But it was Rainier who began to renew her heart after her decades of loss. Even with her growing ability to read what others thought, she could sense no ill motive from him, and, in the beginning, no romantic motive neither. She wondered what impelled his care and attention. He was ten years her junior, but he kept insisting that she was not as old as she claimed. Being a relative newcomer to Paris himself, they explored the city as co-adventurers. Every new taste, sight, or sensation for her was often also new for him. She enjoyed spending time with this man, a rare man that she could not read or manipulate.

Rhiannon was a shy soul, but Rainier helped her find herself. She discovered her voice, learning to speak and listen, instead of eavesdropping. He brought her into a new story as the central character, and not just an outsider in other people's lives. And so she was shocked but pleased, when he suddenly revealed to her his intentions. They were crossing the Pont des Arts, a pedestrian bridge, after spending an afternoon in the Louvre.

"If your mother was here in Paris, I would have asked her permission first," he said. "Will you, Rhiannon Alis Davies, return with me to America and marry me?"

Rhiannon easily accepted his marriage proposal, and the following months would be the happiest of her still short life. They would continue to celebrate in Paris, their personal happiness mixing well with the verve and energy of the city. Lucienne and Emilienne would tearfully bid them adieu as they boarded an ocean liner in the port of Le Havre. They left France on a luxurious cross-Atlantic journey to New York City.

Rhiannon would once again have to face a new world. The Rousseau family had created their wealth during France's industrialization in the 19th Century. As French economic growth slowed in the second half of that century, they immigrated into the United States, settling down in New York City and investing their family wealth into the budding automobile industry. When Rainier was born, the oldest child of Claude and Marie-George Rousseau, he became the heir of the Rousseau wealth.

Although slightly chagrined that their eldest son had found his bride without their counsel, the Rousseaus took Rhiannon into their family. Their wedding was an intimidating but gorgeous occasion at the St. Patrick's Cathedral in Manhattan, and it was Rhiannon's introduction to the society of Rousseau family, friends, and business associates. Unlike with Lucienne and Emilienne, Rhiannon found it difficult to adjust to her new family in New York. With every visitor, she always sensed multi-layered intentions.

Rainier stayed loyal to his wife, and she to him, but he accumulated more responsibility in running the family business. Rhiannon's fears grew as he assumed more and more standing as the Rousseau family head. He officially inherited the Rousseau's holdings when first Claude passed away in 1930, followed by Marie-George in 1935. Rainier became ever absent from their house, isolating Rhiannon at home.

Everybody by this time had started noticing something particularly odd about Mrs. Rainier Rousseau. Although she was supposedly approaching fifty years of age, Rhiannon still looked like a woman half that age. This was before the advent of plastic surgery, and people found it quite peculiar. Her discomfort with the scheming thoughts of Rousseau relatives and hanger-ons caused her to be aloof. This created even more distrust. People became suspicious that the madam of the Rousseau family was so reclusive. Others gossiped about the strange thoughts and ideas that entered their heads when they were around her. Eventually, they whispered to one another about the "Witch of Wales."

This was exacerbated as Rainier grew older and wizened. It was difficult for them to be seen in public together, as people assumed that Rhiannon was a young mistress and not the actual Mrs. Rousseau. Rainier found amusement in his wife's perpetual youth, but he was naïve about the anguish it caused her. He strove to keep the drudgery of his work out of their home, and Rhiannon toiled to keep him oblivious to the drama and chicanery that swirled around her.

Things worsened in 1950, when Rainier suddenly began having difficulty speaking. His speech became slurred. This was an embarrassing ailment to a man who was often in the spotlight. Word spread quickly that something was wrong with him. His doctors were unable to explain what ailed him. Slowly, his health deteriorated further, and he began having difficulty swallowing and eating, despite having started to see a speech therapist. As his health fell, the rumors gained steam. The *surnom* "The Witch of Wales" once again viciously made the rounds.

Rainier began to have occasional and startling outbursts of laughter or crying. He developed an unsettling smile that would appear at inappropriate times. At this point, Rainier stepped back from his work and retreated into the home for rest and treatment. For the rumor mongers, a sordid tale had already been birthed. The tale, woven over afternoon tea, or at swank gatherings of the New York elite, painted Rhiannon as a witch who had beguiled the illustrious scion of the Rousseau clan. Women whispered to each other that she drained life from him to feed her own youth and vitality. People spread allegations that she could cast a plague upon one's mind or inveigle one to do her bidding.

During this time, Rhiannon and Rainier still managed to enjoy each other's company. Even as his speech became incomprehensible, she was able to hear his thoughts. They deepened their communion which each other even while his body started wasting away. He began to have trouble putting on his tie, buttoning his shirt, or tying his shoelaces. He experienced awkwardness as he walked, needing to take care not to stumble or trip. Not before long, his left leg had weakened to the point where his foot would drag along the ground as he walked.

Rhiannon struggled to keep his spirits up as his body betrayed him. He began to withdraw, even from her, which was the worst injury she had to bear. The doctors began to surmise that Rainier possibly had a rare disease called amyotrophic lateral sclerosis. It was a mysterious deterioration of the nervous system which led to muscle degeneration and atrophy. It progressed until death and had no known cure or treatment.

Rainier fell further into depression, and whenever Rhiannon attempted to tap into his mind, the dark thoughts that haunted him would infect her. She began to drift with him. He was eventually bedridden, and she would sit by his side, both of them silent.

Within three years of the onset of his illness, Rainier was dead. This was Rhiannon's fifth and greatest loss.

The family and doctors whisked his body away and prepared funeral arrangements without her input, as she was nearly catatonic in those first weeks after his death. She mostly sat in their bedroom, next to their bed, as if he was still lying there. Her face had taken on a death-like pall. Those who saw her gave her a new *surnom*—"the Blue Ghost of Park Avenue."

From her bedroom crypt, her mind crept in tendrils out into the rest of their mansion, and she clung to existence through the thoughts and ruminations of the relatives and staff who littered the halls. She learned of their plots. Different schemers had different ideas. Some thought it would be best to sue her in court for the estate, after all she was clearly an invalid herself. They feared, and were right, that Rainier had written a will and intended to give her most of the Rousseau wealth. Others insisted she was a witch and that it was best to dispose of her by more deviant means. Like rats, more and more connivers and rascals came into the fold, like vultures hovering over a dying beast.

Rhiannon finally snapped out of her stupor. She smuggled herself out of the house before dawn one day, taking only a few valuables and important documents with her. As the bank opened, she withdrew a significant amount of cash and transferred another large amount into a new account at a different bank. The remaining funds she arranged to have donated to several different charities in the city. Then she drove out of Manhattan, crossing over to New Jersey before heading south through Delaware and Maryland. She fled from the evil storm that was brewing behind her. She would let the relatives and sycophants fight over the scraps of the estate.

Rhiannon drove in a daze, mostly trying to follow the coast. She continued south, driving through Georgia and into Florida. She forged forward into the ocean itself, cruising on the US Route 1 that bridged the Florida Keys archipelago, until she reached the end of the world. Rhiannon Alis Rousseau cast her burdens down, there at the southernmost point of the United States, where for her, life became like death, and death became like life.

Chapter 11

The Things of the Past

JAMES AND AMOS lived in the house in Santa Barbara for several weeks before Hugar made his first phone call to them. He told them it was difficult to get any information from Zachary, but that he was confident he would. James asked him how he was extracting the information, but Hugar said it was not pleasant for him to talk about and changed the subject.

"Have you visited your old home?" Hugar asked.

"No."

"Well, why haven't you? I thought you would have right away."

"I'm afraid."

"I see. I understand, but I tell you—it's safe. Quetzal has gone by it numerous times to check. A family lives there now."

"You think it would be good for me?"

"I think there's no avoiding it. I'll have Quetzal come up and go with you if you'd like."

"I would like that."

"Then it's done, he'll be up this weekend."

Quetzal arrived Saturday morning, and he and James made the short trip to Goleta. Things had changed in the last decades, and he didn't recognize much until they pulled up in front of the house. The fencing around the front yard was gone, and the white exterior was now painted beige, but he recognized the large window in front, and he could see his mother's old bedroom on the second floor. Quetzal walked to the front door and rang the doorbell.

Surprisingly, the woman who answered the door recognized him and shook his hand. It turned out that Quetzal had sold her family the house. James looked at him funny.

"I'm a certified real estate agent," he winked, "a man of many talents."

"I've heard that before," James said.

The woman walked them through the house, but the interior had been redone since James had last been there. A second bathroom and a den had been constructed where his old bedroom used to be. What he really wanted to see was the backyard. They were led through the kitchen to the back, but James found no solace there. The lightning-scorched tree—his secret hiding place— was gone. So were the oak trees where his hammock had hung. The family had dug out everything and put in a swimming pool and garage. Not long after, they thanked the woman and left.

James walked from the house with his head hung low.

"I'm sorry, man," Quetzal said. "We actually thought that this little trip would pep you up. You know, a touch of old memories."

The two of them returned to the little house over the beach. Amos was there with two other people. He had already made some friends from the nearby university. Amos was in a good mood, and he greeted Quetzal with a high five. James heard them making plans for that evening, but he went to his room and went underneath the covers of his bed.

He used to do that, when he was having a bad day, or when he didn't want to face his homework. As a little boy, he liked to sleep as late as he could get away with. When his mother knocked on his door on a Saturday morning, James would pretend he didn't hear her. Sometimes she would leave, and let him sleep. Sometimes she would come in and sit on the edge of his bed. He would then pretend to toss and turn, usually ending up on his side, so his mom could rub his shoulders and kiss him on the cheek.

When he was a bit older, she let him invite friends over, and when it was warm at night, she let them all stay in the backyard. Those were his favorite nights. His friends, Harold and Theodore, usually brought over tents. They would lay the tents out next to his hammock and stick their heads out of the tent opening to talk to him, sometimes until morning. Those were his favorite sunrises. If his mother ever heard them talking, she didn't say, and she never came down to scold them. His friends loved coming over.

When he was sixteen, James became friendly with a girl at school. They happened to have three classes together that spring, and by the end of the semester, they were close friends. Her name was Emma, and she became a fixture in his kitchen. They would sit at the round kitchen table, with James always on the side close to the refrigerator, so he could easily reach inside for some lemonade. His mother made it with club soda instead of water, and Emma couldn't get enough of it while they did schoolwork. She loved coming over, too. If they weren't in the kitchen, she studied while lying in his hammock, and he would sit in a chair.

Over the summer, Emma and her family moved up the coast. She and James tried to keep in touch, although in those days, they could only write letters. They promised each other they would go to the same college, but as time passed, the letters became more infrequent.

He thought of these things, these memories he hadn't touched in a long time. Lying under his covers, he couldn't think of anything but lemonade soda, tents in the summer, and his hammock. There was nothing else to remember. His adult years were stolen from him, and there was nothing beyond his backyard except the burning Mojave sun. He slept like a child, curled under the covers of the bed.

Later, Amos and Quetzal came to wake him.

"Lookie, he's in a fetal position."

"I think he's hiding from us."

"Nonsense, he definitely wants to go."

"Yes, I believe so, too. Let's pull him out."

They pulled at the covers.

"No," James groaned.

He intended to deny their efforts, but they persisted. Short of knocking them unconscious, he had no choice but to succumb. James scowled at them as he got up. He thought they made despicable friends.

Amos had made plans to meet his new friends at a local bar. Quetzal loved the idea and insisted that they take James. Throughout history, it has always been the aspiration and joy of drinking men to take out a friend for his first drink. Amos and Quetzal were full of grins. James was not.

He did not pay attention to where they drove, nor the names of the street, nor the name of the bar. He did not observe the décor of the bar, nor did he notice who the patrons were, nor did he remember the names of Amos's two new friends. Finally, he did not discern what drinks the waitress brought. He simply drank. It was bubbly stuff, very cold in the throat, and he felt it hard in the stomach. It looked like apple juice—did not taste like apple juice at all—and it woke him up. His four comrades were talking about something.

"None of you went to college?" one of Amos's friends was asking.

"No," answered Amos. "I left home twelve years ago to travel. It's just as good as going to university, I say."

"I agree," said Quetzal. "University is a very, very recent phenomenon. Up until a few centuries ago, it was just for the extremely wealthy, and often, for only the religious."

"A few centuries is not recent," said the other friend.

"You're not thinking in a very broad way," Quetzal answered.

"Of course I am," the student answered. "University is all about learning how to think openly—to view the world macrocosmically."

"You only learn how to use big words."

The participants of the conversation all leaned over the table and gestured with their hands. They drew their words in the air as they spoke.

"You're taught from only one point of view."

"Not so, you wouldn't believe how disparate the views of my professors are."

"One point of view—all of them," said Quetzal. "They all come from an American point of view. You are not even getting an inkling of what the other six billion people on earth might think."

"One of my professors is from India."

"Where was he educated?"

"Cambridge, I think."

"England! Virtually the same point of view."

Quetzal excused himself to go to the restroom. James joined the conversation.

"Amos is from England," he said.

"Yes," one of the students laughed. "We could tell right away from his accent."

"I thought I had lost that," Amos said.

"No, not at all, and sometimes you use little British phrases which are wonderful."

"What has always bothered me about Americans is how you use the word 'momentarily,'" Amos said. "Such as, 'the train will arrive momentarily.' Momentarily means 'for just a moment,' doesn't it? How do you Americans have time to get on the train?"

"He's come all this way to find his gr-great-great-grandmother," James said, his voice slurring a little.

They had two pitchers of beer at the table, and he helped himself to another mug. He found that the more he drank, the more interesting the conversation became. Everyone's voices rang loud in his ears. He looked around. Skin was smoother, eyes were brighter, hair more lush. He talked for the sake of being involved.

"Oh, did she live here at one time?" someone asked.

"I think she did, at one point," Amos answered. He changed the subject. "Do you fellows believe in superior beings?"

"What do you mean?"

"Well, I guess, I mean beings, people even, who are just superior in some way—perhaps intellectually, or physically."

"You mean gifted people."

"In a way, I suppose. People who are more advantaged, right from birth."

"The Kennedys," someone said.

"The Rockefellers."

"The Gates, now."

"No, no. Well, just look at my friend here, Jimmy. He's a giant of a man, and I tell you, much older than he looks."

"Yes, I would say he's advantaged. It's in the genes I suppose."

James finished the mug he had poured himself and glanced around the table. Besides Amos, there were now four people, two men and two women. He felt dizzy. He was drunk, he supposed. *Well, good. Every man had a right to do what he wanted, take risks. Replace youthful memories with older ones.* He was drinking, getting drunk, and making new friends in a bar. His head felt like it floated above his neck, which wasn't a bad sensation.

"I can show you what he means," James said, and with one hand he grabbed a corner of the square table and broke it off. A loud crack shot over their heads, and then a triangular piece of two-inch thick wood was in his hand. Amos was slightly aghast, but then he laughed. The women had their hands to their mouths, and the men stared at the wood in his hand.

"Whoa, dude," one of the men said.

James got up from the table to find the restroom. The room spun as he stood, and as he walked forward, he had the same sensation that he received on the moving walkway at the airport. He saw Quetzal near the restroom, talking with a waitress.

"You're not allowed to smoke in here," she said.

"I'm not," he responded.

"Well, I see smoke," she said.

James walked right on by and leaned into the restroom door.

He didn't remember being in the restroom too long. In the next moment, he was back at the table. Quetzal was telling a story, but James couldn't make out what it was about. One of the women kept making eyes at him. He made a decision to talk to her, but then he was outside, standing next to Quetzal's truck.

"Com'on, Jimmy," Amos was saying, "get in the truck."

James wiped a hand across his face and reluctantly got in the truck. They drove back to the house, and he sank into the couch. Quetzal went into the kitchen for a while, and then came out with some coffee. Amos was already asleep on the floor, but Quetzal was talking to James.

"… so I know all about that sort of ambivalence," he was saying. Quetzal reached his slender arms straight up over his head, and unleashed an almost painful-sounding groan as he stretched. As he did so, a thousand wrinkles appeared around his eyes, but they disappeared as he relaxed. "So, let me tell you another story." He took a sip from his cup and started talking.

"Many years ago, the great plumed serpent, Quetzalcoatl, came to a town called Paynala, to visit a noblewoman. This woman was married to the leader of the town, the *Cacique*. Quetzalcoatl intended to seduce and bed her, so that she would bear him a child that would become heir to the Cacique. He did this because his influence had diminished. Quetzalcoatl had disappeared to the East, and the Aztecs who ruled much of Mexico now worshipped other gods.

"He impregnated the noblewoman, and she bore a daughter named Malina. Everyone believed that Malina was the Cacique's child, and so she was now his heir. She lived a good life in Paynala, and her mother would speak to her of her future, insisting that she prepare herself, even at her young age. But a day came when the Cacique died, and Malina's mother would become leader. As her mother was still beautiful and, now, powerful, many suitors came to charm her. One young suitor gained her liking, and they married in an elaborate ceremony. Not before long, she bore her new husband a son. This new Cacique fancied that his son would become heir, and Malina's mother agreed, even though Malina was the firstborn child.

"In the middle of the night, they met with traders from Xicalango, and sent Malina away with them. By the morning, they told all of Paynala that their precious daughter had passed away during the night. The traders traveled to Tabasco, in the Yucatan, and sold Malina to the town's Cacique. It was not difficult for them. Malina was young and very beautiful. She carried herself with pride and strength, despite what her mother had done to her. In the years to come, she showed a skill with languages, mastering several dialects used in the Yucatan.

"While she was in Tabasco, Spanish ships led by Hernan Cortes landed on the coast nearby. The indigenous people were intrigued by Cortes and his guns, as well as the strange deer-like animals his men rode upon. Many began to believe Cortes was Quetzalcoatl returned. After all, Quetzalcoatl had promised to return from the East and defend the people against the Aztec Empire. Cortes was brought gifts to placate and appease him, including twenty daughters of Mexico, one of whom was Malina. Cortes gave the twenty women to his men as slaves. The Spaniards would christen the women, and Malina was renamed Dona Marina.

"Dona Marina soon asserted herself, proving to be different than the others. She began to translate the local dialects for the Spaniards, eventually learning Spanish and becoming Cortes's interpreter. As Cortes and his men conquered the coastal towns, Dona Marina grew to be his most important confidant. She counseled Cortes to make allies of those he conquered. He did so, making allies of the Tlaxcalans, Cempoalans, and others who despised the Aztecs in the west.

"She told him of the vast wealth of Tenochtitlan, the capital of the Aztec Empire. She sang of the heavy rivers of gold snaking down from the mountains into Lake Texcoco, which Tenochtitlan itself was built upon. Cortes became hungry for gold and turned his small army to the west. He had his ships burnt, to prevent mutiny, and after establishing the town of Vera Cruz along the coast, guided the Spaniards and their allies inland.

"They continued all the way to Tenochtitlan. The Aztec emperor sent emissaries with gold, but Cortes was not assuaged. The emperor sent sorcerers, but Cortes was unaffected. They lay siege to Tenochtitlan. The aqueducts were destroyed, and brigantines swept across Lake Texcoco, preventing food and water from reaching the Aztecs. It took months and months, and Cortes suffered many setbacks. But Dona Marina stood by his side, and she continued to reach out to the peoples of Mexico for help against the Aztecs.

"Eventually, the Aztecs began to succumb to the plague, which the Spaniards had brought to Mexico. It was inevitable that their empire would crumble. And so it was done, Cortes captured the golden city of Tenochtitlan. Dona Marina had guided the Spaniards from the coast, all the way to the very heart of Mexico. Because of her, the name Quetzalcoatl is still the name of the greatest god in Mexico."

At this, Quetzal winked.

"What ever happened to Dona Marina?" James asked. He was disappointed that he was beginning to feel sober again.

"She did have a son, named Don Mahin, by Cortes," Quetzal said, his eyes suddenly becoming tired.

"By Cortes?" James asked. "So they fell in love?"

"No, no," Quetzal shook his head. "It was not love. Cortes had Dona Marina married to another man named Juan Jaramillo afterwards. Cortes would return to Spain, where he already had a wife. After that, Dona Marina, she became forgotten, and she died, long, long ago."

In that moment, Quetzal's eyes drooped. He frowned, still gently shaking his head. He closed his eyes and leaned back against the sofa, drifting off to sleep. His story was now done.

Chapter 12

The Blood of Family Is Thick

JAMES LOVED IT when he looked out the window and saw the trees bending in the wind, the sky behind it gray and sad. One couldn't hear anything, being indoors, and it was surreal for him to see those normally passive branches curling about, stretching and shaking in response to the turmoil beyond the glass.

He heard the shuffling of hundreds of leaves complaining at the abuse, but it was a revelation when he stuck his head out the door, and he really did hear the soft roaring of a building storm, the cacophony of limbs and foliage rustling. Growing up in Goleta, such a scene was a break from the everyday monotony of sun and blue sky—it meant for an evening or afternoon that something different was going to happen. It was both ominous and exhilarating.

James was looking out of the front window of the house. It was the first Sunday in October, and a storm was coming.

Amos had come home earlier grumbling. He liked sunny days. They had spent all of September at that house in Santa Barbara, and James had been grateful for the chance to live a little. He had allowed himself to 'frolic' a bit, as Amos had put it. Quetzal had visited several weekends, and the three of them were becoming fairly close. Hugar never visited, but he had kept them updated by phone. Over the past few weeks, he had called to proclaim progress with Zachary. Apparently, Hugar had finally started garnering some information on his mother's whereabouts.

The conditions outside were quickening to the worse. It was the middle of the afternoon but suddenly it became dark. The rains came soon after. Amos settled on the couch with a newspaper, and James sat down with him.

"Holy!" Amos said. He was looking at a picture on the front page of the newspaper. James looked over his shoulder. It was a picture of a building, one that looked very familiar. The very top of it looked blasted open.

Amos read, "The west side of the casino's top floor was severely damaged last night, yet remarkably, no one has been able to verify how it happened."

"Malinche's Palace."

"Yes, look at the picture, it looks like the exterior and roof on that side was blown off."

James took the paper and read the article. Two security guards were found dead on the fortieth floor. A third man by the name of Lamar Kensington, an executive assistant, was found shaking behind a shattered desk. He shook and stammered through the night, the story said, and was taken to a hospital for observation. The alarm system never went off, and authorities were having difficulty even locating anybody at the top of the casino's chain of command. There was no mention of Charlotte.

Amos had gone to the kitchen.

"I called Hugar. He's sending Quetzal up to get us," Amos said when he came back. "He hadn't read the paper yet, but he sounded upset when I told him."

"Why? Isn't it safe up here?"

"He didn't say, but I think it's Kensington. The old man was loyal to Honus and Hugar. He knows about this house. If he'd said anything, Charlotte would sniff us out in a jiffy."

They waited. A drive from Santa Monica would take two hours, and Amos spent much of that time drinking hot tea and pacing the living room. Outside, the winds were blowing hard, and the rain dribbled against the windows from time to time. Large, hard drops drummed on the roof and pounded upon the foliage outside. Looking through the sliding balcony doors, James watched the ocean churning for a time, as if it was in a war with the heavens. It was almost evening, and with the clouds above, it was getting dark. The living room was becoming warm, and it shrunk inwards as if a pressure came from all sides.

"I think someone's here," James said.

Amos was sweating. "I don't hear the truck," he said. He looked out a side window. "Nothing in the driveway."

There came knocking on the door—tap-tap-tap—an unnatural sound in the midst of nature's wailing.

Amos stayed where he was, so James walked over to the door. Someone was scratching on the door from the outside. He looked through the peephole but saw no one. Amos came over to the front window and peered out. He grimaced and jumped back slightly.

"Don't open it," he gasped.

But James took a breath and opened the door.

A woman in white knelt on the floor. From the look of her arms, she was emaciated. Limp, wet hair fell all around her face, and James could not yet see her eyes. Slowly, she stood, her bones shaking under her skin with the effort. Her hair looked brown and was matted to the front of a taut, chalky visage. With a hand, she shifted aside some of the hair covering her face. It took James another moment to see her for who she was.

"Charlotte," he said. His voice caught at the very back of his throat.

"Yes-s-s," came a small cry.

A force suddenly hit James's chest, and he lost his breath. He tried to resist and stand his ground, but his legs buckled, and he was impelled backwards into the living room. He glimpsed Amos walking backwards from the window, grasping his chest. Charlotte shuffled slowly upon the floor and into the house. The room became very hot, and the air felt like it was boiling as it was inhaled into James's lungs. He could feel a slight chill coming from the balcony, so he crawled towards it. Amos met him there. Amos's eyes were wide. Charlotte stood in the middle of the room, looking at them sadly.

"My brother," she rasped.

"We don't have him," James managed to say. The walls of the room were curving outwards now, as if Charlotte was exerting a force from the center where she stood. Her hair was dry now, and once again flaming red.

"I said we would not be polite, this time." She spoke slowly, all the while gazing at and through James.

"The casino—was that you?" he asked.

And here Charlotte smiled, her teeth yellow beneath her thin red lips. "No, it was him," she said, and she leered and nodded behind her. James looked towards the front door.

"No one's there," he said, but then he noticed the shadow. It crept in from the door and soon covered half the room—ceiling, floor, and walls.

"Jimmy, the shadow," Amos whispered beside him.

"I see it."

"You see?" Charlotte said. She shuffled to the left, away from the center of the room. "Let me introduce my father."

"Amargat," Amos said, but he was drowned out by a sudden rumbling. The shadow had covered nearly the entire living room, except for a strip where James and Amos sat against the balcony sliding doors. Outside, thunder rolled.

Right in the center of the room, blackness grew from light, and a dark, convulsing thing expanded, like a black heart beating. Charlotte stood to the side, looking at it with fondness, and it grew until it filled half the room. James stared at it. He saw that it was a rolling ball of black feathers. Then, quick as a lightning flash, it filled the breadth of the room.

A wall of the black feathers now existed in front of James, leaving him little room, but then it moved itself, and curled upwards, like a stage curtain pulled up, and gigantic black eyes revealed themselves. He stifled a scream, as for a second, he thought it was Borus, but he saw it was a man's face, not a bull's— a bronze face, with a black mustache over a wide mouth. A giant of a man was now crouched in the room—his body was dark and naked, and he was muscled like an ape. From his back, and filling the room, black-feathered wings sprouted.

"The Blackbyrd," James muttered.

Amargat reached out and clutched James around his torso with one immense hand. The black feathers ran down his back and down his arms.

"MY SON," he said. James felt Amargat's voice rumbling down his spine.

"I don't have him," James grunted. He could hardly talk, as his ribs were compressed inward.

"It's true, the statue is not here," Amos said, but he was ignored.

Charlotte ducked underneath Amargat's face, and she knelt on the floor in front of James.

"We come for him, that is all," she said. "We leave with him, or with your corpses."

"YOUR CORPSES," came the rumbling.

Amargat's grip tightened. James had no choice; with all the strength he had, he pried Amargat's thumb and fingers apart, then twisted out of his grip. He kicked the giant's palm away. Amargat's hand was brushed back by the force, but he quickly recovered. James fell to the floor, and before he could react, Amargat brought his fist forward and struck a mighty blow.

For that split second, James heard nothing, and time slowed. The impact of the blow knocked him backwards, shattering the glass sliding door behind him, and he saw the small dark room retreat from him, along with the bronze and white faces of Amargat and Charlotte and the cascade of devastated glass. In that moment, he continued flying backwards, smashing through the wooden balcony guard—he saw the wood splinter and fly around him—and he then fell down, the charcoal sky above him, the falling rain coming down in voluptuous drops. He landed with a thud in the sands of the beach below. His eyes strained to stay open, and he glimpsed Amargat explode from the house, his black wings spread, blocking the sky. As James lost consciousness, he thought that Amargat would crush him into the ground. And it all went dark.

In the living room, Amos could breathe again, and as he looked around, the lines and corners of the room straightened out and the shadows were lifted from throughout. Charlotte stood near him still, but now she did not look so menacing. She wore a widow's pall, now that she was divested of her father's presence.

"I asked before, without my father," she said. She slowly moved to the couch, and in a movement that seemed too casual for the circumstance, dipped backwards and sat.

The strange magnetism of the floor relented, and Amos managed to stand. He crept onto the balcony, littered with glass and splintered wood, and looked up at the sky. He did not see Amargat. Down below, James was unconscious, or dead. He could hear squawking somewhere above the house.

"He will die," Charlotte said. She sat still on the worn cushions of the couch, eyes fixed forward. Her face was a muddle of young and old features. Her skin pale and thin, but taut, her eyes weary but burnished. She was not unpretty, but Amos thought her ghastly, even before her recent deterioration.

"Jimmy, or your brother?" Amos asked, sidling to the far wall across from her.

"Perhaps both."

"It needn't be so. I can give you your brother, and your father can leave Jimmy alone."

"You do not have my brother."

Amos paused for a moment before responding, "I can guarantee your brother, but I do ask … a favor."

Charlotte said nothing.

"You will understand my request, for I can see how you yearn for your brother," Amos said. "I have searched for a loved one, much longer than you have searched for Zachary."

Amos had waited long enough, as he toiled for Hugar the past few years. He knew opportunity when it presented itself and now saw that his fate and James's crossed in that small living room they shared. In coming to Hugar, he had chosen paths that were hidden, rugged, and now, he would leave on another such harsh trail. He spoke firmly, his words coming deliberately, sometimes pleading, sometimes complimenting, feeling that this was an audition, this proposition to Charlotte, and that soon, he would finally be received—lovingly borne into that world he coveted—*her* world.

He rushed his words, stumbling here and there, but Charlotte would nod, still fixated on some point through and beyond him, and at some point she stood, nodded again, and whispered to him a few words of destination. He extracted a yellowed letter, still earnestly imploring. Then, the letter was gone, and so was Charlotte. He was alone, his shoulders rising and falling as his words dribbled off his lips into silence. Amos stood there a long while, a salesman who could not believe his good fortune, his eyes adopting Charlotte's far-off glaze. Eventually, he regained the wherewithal to find the rear door of the house, and he walked down the wooden steps to the beach below.

James was lying on the beach, his arms and legs splayed limply in the sand. He was unconscious but still breathing. Soon, Quetzal arrived and joined them on the beach.

"Who did this?" he asked.

"Amargat," Amos said.

"I've heard that name," Quetzal said, looking concerned.

He and Amos carried James back up to the house and then into Quetzal's truck. They drove that evening down to Santa Monica.

The next morning, with daylight coming through the blinds, James woke to find Hugar sitting at the foot of his bed.

"Good morning," James said. He winced as he attempted to prop himself up on an elbow.

Hugar turned to face him and smiled. It was a forced smile, meant to rally his soldier. "Good morning, James. It's *kismet* that you endure upon this world, if from Amargat's palm you escape."

"He was imposing."

"It gives me pride to see you have such strength and self-possession."

James did not think it was such an impressive feat. He simply reacted, as he had been doing the entire time since he was freed. "I just used whatever strength I had, got free."

"Oh, if it was that easy. I don't think even our father could free himself of the crippling fear that Amargat shackles onto a being."

"I didn't do much. I was knocked out, but I think Amos somehow drove them off."

Hugar looked down at his hands cupped in his lap. "Oh, I don't think he drove them off," he said.

He stood up and walked over to the windows. Sunlight, the color of warm butter, came in between the blinds and painted him with glowing bands across his face and shoulders. He looked, a bit nervously, out the windows.

"Is something wrong, Hugar?"

"Our friend Mr. Gillett has gone off," he said. "I found my office at the restaurant broken into, and the trogon statue is gone."

"And you think Amos took it?" James asked. "Now why would he do that?"

"Oh yes, it's clear," said Hugar. "You are knocked unconscious by the Blackbyrd, but somehow they leave you without further harm. Amos is untouched, and the very next morning, the trogon statue, with Zachary in it, is gone."

"I see."

"Amos is a man with his own motivations," Hugar continued. "I thought he was loyal enough to me, but when opportunity presented itself, he switched his allegiance."

"I don't really blame him," James said. "He and I, we want the same thing. We both want to find a bit of our past. We both want to know where we came from."

Hugar and James both knew it. Amos could no more resist taking the statue for his own purposes, than he could resist picking up his leather bag that day in London when he walked away from his old life.

"What is he, Hugar?" James asked. "I mean, Amargat."

Hugar sighed. "Amargat, he is …"

"Is he some sort of devil?" James ventured.

"That is what some people would say," Hugar said. "Mr. Gillett would say he is a god."

"And so is he right?"

"Is Amargat a deity to be worshipped? No. Even Amargat would scoff at that suggestion."

"Then what is he?"

"The word that you would understand," Hugar explained, "is angel."

James stood up and paced around the room. He became agitated and clenched his fists, nearly punching the wall. He stopped himself short.

"You mean, I just did battle with an angel of heaven?" he asked. "Something as sinister and grotesque as that Blackbyrd thing— that's an angel?"

"Whatever his title, he was stripped of it long ago."

"And Father!" James shouted. "What is Father? Is he some grotesque thing too?"

"James Henry Worth! Calm down."

"Well, tell me! What does that make me and you? We're like demon children or something!"

"Sit down, James!" Hugar commanded. He pointed a finger at James and waited. In the dimly lit room, Hugar suddenly loomed large. His shadow stretched and filled half the room. Breathing heavily, James submitted and sat back down.

"The old civilizations," Hugar said, "called them Watchers. They had been keeping watch over men, before men could write or keep history. Our father Honus, Amargat, and the *Azâzêl* of whom Zachary and Charlotte spoke, they were merely three out of two hundred. These Watchers and their children performed great, and sometimes terrible, feats on the earth. Men took notice, passing stories of these heroes of old down through generations. Many of these tales spoke of gods and other divine beings. These stories make up a vast number of the myths and legends still being retold today. But now, this late in history, only a handful of Watchers still walk the earth. You and I, Charlotte, Zachary, Margaret, Quetzal— we are offspring to these few remaining Watchers."

He stopped and turned to James. "But I beg you, young James, be patient. Learn your heritage slowly. Otherwise, it is too much to bear, and you will become corrupt. You will make the wrong decisions."

James nodded. He looked at his palms. The lines on his palms, his hands, his flesh—they were part of something he did not understand.

"So, what do we do now?" he asked.

"Good, that's the spirit," Hugar said, his cheerful smile returning. "We must focus on the tasks at hand."

James looked up at Hugar, expecting his half-brother to say something, to form a solution. But they both fell silent a while, pondering which paths remained.

Chapter 13

A Very Old Man

JAMES WAS ALONE again. Hugar had instructed him to fly back to Las Vegas. The plan was to look there first for his cousins, or for Amos. Hugar was going to try to dig up some information, perhaps an address for Zachary and Charlotte in Las Vegas. But James was lying alone in a motel room, on a sad street that was not Las Vegas Boulevard, but one of its forgotten cousins that crossed it. It was one of the streets leading west or east, away from paradise and into somber neighborhoods.

This was his favorite thing to do, lying on a stiff bed, the sheets tucked in over the top of mattress like a tight shirt. He found the temperature of motel rooms pleasing, not like the blistering Mojave day or the chilly dustiness of the Mojave night. The four walls of the room insulated him, blocking out the mess of the world and not allowing anyone outside of that space to see him—not allowing anyone to see the *freak* that was inside.

Several days passed in his motel room. James was in his old habits again. The rifling through of lost memories, the varnishing of hazy thoughts, and the endless flow of barely sustained consciousness seized him once again, now that he was without the ministration of others. Weeping engaged him at whim, upon the contemplation of his mother, or merely on the trail of a random memory that harbored no meaning to him. Whatever strength saved him from Amargat was reflexive. He now needed a decisive manner, a cognizance of the world outside his mind and the actions it took to send ripples through it.

On the third day, James grew hungry, a deep hollow hunger groaned its presence within James's body and rattled its call up his throat. He slid heavy legs off his bed and went to open the blinds. It was daylight.

He stumbled across the street to a diner, where he ate a hefty meal, and as his hunger disappeared, a sense of guilt and dread replaced it. He was supposed to call Hugar after he got into Las Vegas. He privately cursed himself. Emilia Worth had always been a woman of common sense; she always knew what to do, no matter the situation. James used to admire that. Even when she was stumped, she would give it a go, and step-by-step, she got to an answer.

After finishing his meal, he called Hugar, waited out the older man's ranting and protestations, and then asked if there was any new information.

"I have an address," Hugar said. "This is the house that Zachary and Charlotte use when they're in Vegas. Let's hope that it'll get us somewhere."

The address was on Coley Avenue, west of the 15 Freeway which split Las Vegas in half. James had waited until dark and had the taxi driver drop him off down the street. He walked with his hands in his pockets down the sidewalk, hearing mostly the drone of cars on nearby roads and the usual symphony of crickets. A man was shouting in one of the houses, but James saw nobody, and the ruckus was strangely fitting to this particular street as the sky darkened from blue to black. He reached the address.

The house was modest, with a nearly flat roof with green trim and a chain-linked fence around the front. The lights were all out, and James hoped that no one was home. He didn't hesitate in front of the gate, walking right through and up to the front door, where he pretended to fiddle with nonexistent keys before grabbing the doorknob and leaning in with his shoulder. He heard the cracking of wood, and the door gave.

Minutes later, he was in one of the bedrooms, searching through a desk, flipping through a few folders. He found nothing except some photocopied articles on astrology, a telephone bill, and a gentlemen's magazine. He guessed that it was Zachary's room. After rummaging through his closet, James headed out to the kitchen, attracted by a dining table cluttered with paper and forms. Mostly, it was faxes of invoices and timesheets.

He went to a second bedroom, this one with pink and red bedding. He opened drawer after drawer. He looked in her closet. On the shelving in the closet, he found a tin box. Inside of the box were a stack of postcards. There must have been about fifty postcards in total. As he shuffled through them, he saw that they were all sent from Arizona. Different postcards displayed landscapes from the Sonoran Desert, cacti and mountains, and also well-manicured grass lawns from a city named Wickenburg.

He browsed through a few of them. They were all short, composing of only one or two lines each. The writer's cursive was impeccable. He noticed that they were mostly dated around Christmas of each year, and they were all signed, "Your father." He flipped through the postcards. Most of them didn't have a return address, but on one postcard from December 1993, it said, simply: "My new address. Please write back." A street address from Wickenburg, Arizona, was printed neatly.

James kept that postcard and quickly exited the house, thanking his luck that no one came home. He continued on from Las Vegas, speaking with no one, having no reason to speak.

The next afternoon, he flew into Phoenix, using some of the cash that Hugar had given him. For some reason, he decided not to check in with Hugar by phone. From Phoenix, he went by taxi fifty miles northwest to Wickenburg. It was an old town, founded in the late nineteenth century, and still clung, at least in a superficial way, to its Old West roots. Guest ranches catered to visitors who wandered in. Smiling hosts with name tags proffered cowboy hats and what passed for Old West friendliness. In its early days, it lured miners in search of gold in the mountains just to its north, while farmers and ranchers were enticed by the fertility of the Hassayampa River flood plain. Nowadays, its gentle western atmosphere attracted mainly tourists and retirees, and its weekly newspaper boasted that it was one of the nation's "leading retirement communities."

It was a peculiar place for Amargat to be, but this address was now all James had. It was his only path to Amos. He missed his friend. James felt no ill will at Amos for taking the statue. Perhaps if he could find him, he would tell him so.

Dusk was fast approaching when he found the place. It was a small ranch-style home on the outskirts of the town. He hesitated a bit in front of the house. It was quiet, and the landscape, riddled with shrubs and foothills, demanded his attention. The land rose and fell gently, marked here and there by ridges and peaks. The town rested on the base of a riparian mountain range, now looming over the darkening town. It was an easy place to be forgotten, here in the embrace of the hills, surrounded by old rivers and lakes, the past so evident in the present. He stood awhile and breathed in the air, untainted by the smell of exhaust and gasoline, plastic and rubber, steel and paint, and the myriad other scents produced by a modern city with all its self-medications. He smelled the earth.

Behind him, the front door of the house opened, and a warm light spilled out upon his feet.

"Ah, what a pleasant surprise," came a voice.

James turned and saw the silhouette of a tall, slim man. The man's arms were spread out in front of him, and he stepped aside and waved James into the house. As he did so, James saw his face in the light. It was a tanned face, with a thin mustache stretched over a wide smile. His hair was black and close-cropped.

"Please, come in," Amargat said.

James walked silently into the house. He came into a cozy room, lit only by candles on a low table in the center and on the wood-panel walls. There were no chairs, but thick rugs lay scattered throughout the floor. The room was windowless and one wall was lined with shelves low to the ground. Dozens of rocks and gems of all sizes were on the shelves, some were rugged and some polished.

"Please sit," Amargat said.

James sat on an intricate rug next to the shelving. It was rectangular, with a hexagonal Herati diamond design in the middle and beveled corners inside the main border. Amargat briefly left the room and came back with two mugs. He placed one near James on the lone table and kept the other for himself.

"Delicious," he said. "Please try."

James reached over with a long arm and took the mug, holding it in his large hands. The drink was thick and cold, a mixture of different exotic fruits he didn't recognize. He felt more at peace than he expected, sitting across from a being of frightening power. But it was a warm house, nestled away between the homes of gold miners' descendants and the mountains they used to roam. He suffered no fear.

Amargat sat a mere four feet from him, shrunk now to a less imposing figure than during their first meeting. The Watcher leaned back against the wall, occasionally sipping his drink, smiling always, his eyes crinkling at the edges into crow's feet. James reveled in the silence for a while, wondering if this drink was Amargat's attempt at an apology for their first meeting. James imbibed it, waiting for the Watcher to speak.

"You are here to find out what happened to your friend, Amos ... and my son, Zachary."

James eyed the old man, perhaps a bit too suspiciously. Amargat held a steady gaze on James. He was in no rush to continue the conversation even after bringing the subject up so abruptly.

"No worries, James. You fear that I hold your trespass against my son against you. But, I think the two sides have trespassed against each other. Or perhaps, it can be argued that Zachary's offenses against you were more grievous. No, let me correct that. My children's offenses against you were certainly more grievous."

"They relished in the pain they inflicted in me for forty years, sir," James finally responded. "They are cannibals."

"Cannibals?" Amargat asked. "They are not human, and neither are you. No, you are different. My Charlotte and Zachary, they descend from two of the old fathers, dear boy. You, only one."

"Does that excuse what they did to me?"

"No, but power does," Amargat said. "In ancient days, disputes were resolved through battle. If one was wronged, the natural recourse was to avenge that wrong through brute force. If one was not strong enough to do so, then the violation must be accepted as part of the natural order of power. My children needed me, and now I have stepped in to stand by their side. I am their champion and advocate. And, by my estimation, any ill will between the two of us has been neutralized." He ever so slightly cocked an eye at James. "Or has it been, my dear boy?"

"I have no wish to battle you."

"Excellent. In fact, dear child, I have much to be thankful for. You have, inadvertently, unintentionally, but nonetheless, you have reunited me with my children. In the hour of their greatest need, my children turned back to me. They needed their father again, at long last."

Amargat smiled at James and lifted his mug in a friendly gesture.

"Now, we move on to the matter of your friend. Let me just say he acted rightly, by agreeing to assist us in the matter of Zachary. I should hope that you're not seeking to do him harm?"

Once again, his scrupulous gaze.

Amargat stood up and walked over to the low shelf. Surveying his collection, he took a small silver tray from the shelf. He picked up a simple gray rock. Pulling a small black pouch from his pocket, he put the rock inside of it and cinched it. He then slowly put a few of the other stones and gems on the tray.

"Here is a gift, and an answer, for you to peruse after you leave." Amargat handed the black pouch to James, and then he sat back down, a look of content on his face. He inspected the gems that remained on the tray. "This is a small part of my collection. Precious, every one of them." He picked up a small crystal gem and handed it to James. It was vivid red on one half and blue on the other. "Tourmaline, bi-colored," Amargat said. "Do you feel anything?"

"No," James said. "Just a slight blurring of my vision." He gave the gem back. Amargat held it in a palm for a moment, caressing it with his thumb.

"You never did meet her, did you? Ah, you are less than a century old, I forget." he said. "Helena, my wife. She left this earth when the children were born." He handed James an unfinished ruby. "I keep my memories in these jewels. Some of them are as old as I am. Without them, I wouldn't remember anything from the olden days."

A bitterness came to James's mouth, and he reflexively clenched the ruby in his palm. A searing pain laced his torso. He dropped the stone on the rug. "Charlotte," he said.

"Yes, my daughter. A good girl, generally. Slightly spiteful. She didn't tell me who you were. I wouldn't have been so … brusque."

Amargat browsed over his collection for a while. His hand paused over some, touching the surfaces. He eventually chose a purplish-red gem and offered it. "A diamond," he said. "Very rare in this color range." At first, James sensed nothing, but gradually, a heat grew in his chest. It spread and intensified. A prism of light burst in his head as he closed his eyes. The longer he held the gem, the angrier he became. He gnashed his teeth and his breath stopped in his lungs. Amargat reached over and easily pried the diamond from his hand.

"My father," James said. His eyes stung from fresh tears. "It was vague at first. I never met him, but then came the anger."

"You have strong feelings, though you never met him." Amargat scrutinized James for several moments. "But I sense that neither of us want to talk about—, hm, what name does he go by in these days?"

"Honus Roosevelt."

"Indeed. Some of us old-timers like to—how do you say it nowadays—um, yes, *update* our names as the centuries pass by. Some of us try to keep current, but I say it's a useless exercise. Already, the name Honus Roosevelt sounds a little, hm, outdated, wouldn't you say? Why bother with such useless exercise?"

Amargat stood up and went to the adjoining room. He came back with a simple wooden box. It had no paint, varnish, or finish of any kind on it. The wood looked almost rotten. But it was hard and smooth to the touch—petrified, almost like stone. He took off the lid, and then pulled out a small amount of yellowed fabric. Finally, he gently lifted out a small stone, cupped in his left palm. With absolute care, he held it towards James. The old man waited with just the slightest bit of concern in his brow.

When James put out both hands to receive the stone, Amargat said, "Careful." And then he put the stone in James's hands.

The rock was small, like a shooting marble. It was dark like charcoal and very porous. It was very light, and James was sure he could crush it into dust easily.

"Just let it rest in your hands, now close your eyes and just breathe."

James did as he was told.

A breeze was blowing ever so gently, from where he didn't know. He noticed it first upon his right ear. Something brushed along his thighs, his calves. He stopped walking. The soil underneath his bare feet was soft, but not wet. He dug his toes into the ground and felt the soothing earth squish between his toes and caress the bottom of his feet. He reached out both hands and felt the tall grass that came up to his waist. He slowly moved his right thumb and finger up along a stalk. It was not ridged or sharp, but soft, pliant. A scent of lavender teased his nostrils, and he wondered if he should collect a bundle.

He had nowhere to be. Food was waiting somewhere back in a shaded hut. Somewhere waiting for him were berries and melons, and beans that were ground into a paste and seasoned with spices from the nearby land. There was plenty. He needed to just walk the land until he was hungry, and then he would go to the hut and eat.

The warmth of the sun washed against his shoulders, his arms, his chest. He decided he would stand there a while, soft soil between his toes, the dancing grass about his waist, the sun upon his face, and him, lightly grasping at the wind between his fingers. He would do so until he felt the earliest pangs of hunger in his throat, and then he would make the journey home.

James opened his eyes to see Amargat staring intently at him. The old man had a slight smile on his face.

"That is my favorite."

James carefully gave the stone back. "I can see why."

Amargat looked to the side and contemplated something for a while. The lines along his forehead and jaw undulated slightly as he thought.

"Can you imagine a life without burden?" he asked. "A life without expectation, or even time, only the rising and the setting of the sun. The waxing and waning of the moon. The sudden appearance of babies, infants, who grow taller and taller. They become men and women, first taut of skin, but eventually beset by wrinkles, which deepen and deepen. These men and women receive new names as they gain respect or notoriety, serve new functions, among their peers, but they are not described as being of a certain age. There are no words for years, or even months. You see these changes happening in the sky, and in the space around you, and they give you a rudimentary understanding of change, although not necessarily time. No calendars, not in those days. Snow, rain, droughts, and floods, they came and went. But no division of time into the seconds, minutes, and hours of today. No language to describe whether time passes quickly, or slowly, whether things are being done according to the dictatorial whim of time. No appointments and deadlines and prioritization of tasks and projects.

"It was like this for hundreds of thousands of years. More time, boy, than you will ever comprehend. But wherever you may reside in this universe, there will always arrive some scale of violence from the outside. Men and women would gladly spend their entire lives in leisure except that some other would come along and cut their heads off, take their cattle and grain, and their innocence.

"So we were there to help the ones that were the chosen children. Some today would say that they were arbitrarily designated for salvation. But it was not as crude as that. We counseled, we guided. We watched, and we acted when necessary."

He paused and looked into James's eyes.

"I can see that you have already heard of the Watchers, yes?" he asked.

"A little," James answered.

Amargat grew silent for a while. He sat cross-legged on the floor and contemplated something. James grew restless, and soon, his drink was empty.

"I admit to you, we made mistakes. But those of us who still linger on this world, we are the ones who attempted to rectify what had already been done. I, for my part, have long stayed out of the fray. And what has this world become? The people think themselves advanced and civilized. Worthless words that suggest they have reached a higher state of understanding. But they are so far ... so far. It only means they can bring violence in newer and more devastating ways.

"Scant remnants of the older ways cling onto life here in this world. Scatterings of folk who somehow evaded our reckless education, and in their language, they still lack the words for structured, unforgiving time. But even they are threatened. Just as we who once watched had educated and spoiled the early children, even these remnants are invaded by educators, researchers, evangelists who seek to destroy the only last remaining bastions of peace in this world. We shall never learn."

"What did you mean," James asked, "when you said earlier that you made mistakes?"

Amargat looked away, off to a corner of the room, but not really looking at anything. James was getting adjusted to the elder's agonizing way of letting time pass. Amargat seemed to be still trying to recapture that life of timeless existence. Neither calendar, clock, nor a waiting visitor would stir him to move faster than he wanted. He took a slow sip from his mug.

James withdrew into his own thoughts. He wondered if the old Watcher really had been there hundreds of thousands of years before, walking among the barefoot men and women who wandered the earth in small splinters of family and extended family. He knew nothing of prehistoric times. All that remained were crude drawings on cave walls, the occasional discovery of pottery and tool fragments, or human fossil, either bits of bone or, more sensationally, a body preserved in ice or mud.

The two men at that moment made eye contact. The older man had a hint of amusement in his eyes and on his lips, as if he had a secret that he could neither keep, nor divulge to another.

"Take it for what it is," he shrugged. "I speak truth, but it matters not. It benefits you not to hear of such old things."

James wished that he had the words to coax more out of the Watcher, but he was not one who was elegant with words. And Amargat was firm. The old man would not say more, would not budge. The conversation suddenly was over and Amargat moved lightly and quickly. The mugs and plates, the wooden box, and the tray of stones were gone and stowed away.

James stood up, his mind still half-tucked away in some cave a hundred thousand years prior. He absent-mindedly shuffled toward the door and mumbled a thank you and good-bye. He walked from the house, ruminating over the possibilities of the far past. He imagined Amargat in his great winged form, stomping through fields of many millennia ago and saw vague images of a tall, thin man pontificating by firelight to crude-minded people of a past age. He thought of many more things, and it wasn't until early the next morning that he broke out of his reverie. He was walking along the side of a highway. James didn't get the information he wanted from Amargat. But his head was infinitely full of other thoughts.

Chapter 14

Up the Mountain He Goes

HE TRIED TO HITCHHIKE, just as he had learned from Amos those weeks before. James walked along the highway and stuck his thumb out. A dozen cars drove right by without slowing down, until finally, a man stopped.

"Where are you headed?" asked the man.

"Los Angeles," James said.

"You're going the wrong way, son," the man laughed. "Get on the other side of the road."

An hour later, James managed to get picked up by a family in a minivan. They were a lively, curious bunch and tried to start conversation with him, but he was in no mood to talk about anything. They left him alone, and he settled into the back for a long nap.

By that afternoon, they were making their way through the Los Angeles Basin. James had awoken but was still in a daze from his encounter with Amargat. His head was spinning. So it wasn't until late in the afternoon that he remembered the gift. Reaching into his pocket, he pulled out the small black pouch and took out the small gray stone. He rubbed it between his index finger and thumb.

Suddenly the sensation of falling hit him. His stomach lurched. His vision cleared, and he looked down. Trees and mountains were far below him. He was flying. He flailed his arms, but they wouldn't respond. Instead, he had white wings that were spread on either side, stroking against the wind. He dove earthward, gliding in a great big spiral. He looked again below him and saw a house, nestled amongst the trees on the slope of the mountain. It rose to him, coming closer and closer until he reached out his great taloned feet and landed on the edge of the house's roof.

Bits of information seeped into his brain. The house sat in the San Gabriel Mountains, off of the Angeles Crest Highway. It was near a city called La Canada Flintridge, north of downtown Los Angeles. The information, and the vision, stopped abruptly. He held the small gray stone between his finger and thumb. James looked out the window of the minivan. They were on the 10 Freeway, the highway that brought him in June back to the Pacific Ocean. He looked north and barely saw a range of mountains through the haze and smog. His destination was somewhere in those mountains.

The family dropped him off in downtown Los Angeles. He spent a few hours trying to find a bus route north. It was nearly impossible, as the signage at the bus stops were indecipherable to him. He didn't know enough about Los Angeles to be able to navigate through its many bus lines. He stopped a man who was riding on a bicycle and asked if he would be willing to sell it. The man laughed at him, but James pulled out whatever money he had in his pockets. They counted $217. The man pursed his lips and then said, "Sure, take it."

The man gave him directions toward the city of La Canada Flintridge. James hopped onto the bike and road northeast along Broadway. He rode past the wholesale jewelers of the downtown area, past the LA Times building and civic buildings in the area around 1st Street. Staying on Broadway, he cut through Chinatown and then went by Elysian Park.

This city never ends, he thought. He had to stop every few blocks to get oriented, or to ask for more directions from pedestrians. He made his way over to Figueroa Street, continuing toward the northeast. Palm trees lined his path as he rode through Highland Park, a picturesque area between the Mt. Washington, San Rafael, and Monterey Hills that was also one of the oldest settled areas in Los Angeles.

As he turned north and biked past the 134 Highway, the community grew more affluent, and he began to pass country clubs and golf courses, as well as the Rose Bowl. Much of the way was hilly, and by this point, James's shirt was completely soaked with sweat.

He pressed forward, the pounding in his heart growing harder and louder as he progressed further toward his destination. He turned left briefly onto Foothill Boulevard, and then shortly after, he turned right onto Angeles Crest Highway. Immediately before him, even with the darkening sky, he saw the green and brown San Gabriel Mountains looming. If he was going to get where he wanted to go, James would have to conquer the mountain roads on a creaky old bike. He had already biked for hours, and hours more waited.

He stopped and pulled the little stone out, experiencing again the vision of the house in the mountain. The path forward became clearer to him, and he began to follow his gut.

The straight roads of the city soon gave way to the curving and looping highway that climbed into the Angeles National Forest. He pedaled forward, not allowing himself to think. He focused on the rhythmic exertion of his legs and feet. He now stood up on his bike as he pedaled uphill. As the highway entered the forests, what remained of daylight quickly disappeared. He kept moving, guided by his instincts, and his eyes soon adjusted enough to the dark for him to barely make out the road in front of him.

He biked in the blackness for hours more, sometimes climbing up a slope, sometimes cruising downhill. His legs didn't grow weary, and his heart's beating remained stable and strong. He was no longer sweating, since much of his body fluid had evaporated.

Suddenly, he veered to the left and pulled off the main highway. He was very close; he could feel it. About ten minutes later, he stopped. He could see almost nothing by this point. Away from the city lights, nothing holds back the blackness of night. But he felt *it* there to his left. He got off the bike and walked towards the trees. Sure enough, a small footpath allowed him to continue away from the road. It wasn't long before he stood in front of a small cabin. No light emanated from within so it stood before him as a black hulk. He decided not to risk bothering anyone, but he couldn't stand much longer. He let the bike fall to the ground and felt his way around the building. In the back on a small porch was a rocking chair. He sat down and immediately fell asleep.

He woke up to someone punching him in the arm.

"Get up, you big brute. That's my chair."

He opened his eyes and saw a familiar face.

"Amos? It's you."

"Yeah, you found me," Amos said. "Now get out of my chair."

"This is your chair? You live here?"

James stood up groggily. Amos brushed past him and sat down into the chair. He smiled as he started rocking back and forth.

"No, but it belongs in my family, at least. And besides, I was here first. I've been coming here for the past three days. How did you find me anyway?"

"I found Amargat. He helped me."

"You? You found Amargat? How did you manage to do that?"

"Hugar got an address for Zachary and Charlotte. I went there and found Amargat's address."

"Well, I'll be," Amos said. "Wait, you didn't tell Hugar about this place, did you?"

"No. I was supposed to check in with him yesterday. But I haven't."

"Are you going to tell him?"

"Why, is this your hideaway or something?"

"No."

"Then why are you here?"

"First promise me you won't tell Hugar, or Quetzal, about this place."

James thought about it for just a second. Then he said, "Everybody needs a safe place to go. Sure, I won't say anything."

Amos stopped rocking. He leaned over toward James and smiled.

"I may have finally found her. My great-great-grandmother, Rhiannon Alis Davies. After years of serving Hugar, and his empty promises, I think this is the place."

"Charlotte helped you?"

"Yes. I have to give Hugar that much credit. If it wasn't for his crackpot plans, I never would have met these beings who have real power—real ability—who could help me."

"And in return you gave them the statue with Zachary?"

"Well, sure. That's what they came for." He looked guiltily at James. "They would have killed you, Jimmy! Com'on, I probably saved your life, if anything. Besides, Hugar wasn't getting anywhere with Zachary."

"And have you met her then?" asked James.

"No, I've come here for the last three days, and I haven't seen her. But I've peeked inside, and someone lives here. They must be away. I'm going to keep coming back until I meet whoever it is."

"Do you have water?" asked James.

"Yeah, sure, in the car." He tossed a set of keys to James.

James took his time walking back down the road. Amos had parked his car up the road a bit where there was some space off on the side. Amos had a few bottles of water in the car, and James finished off two of them quickly. He wasn't sure if he should wait in the car and give Amos some privacy. He imagined for a moment what it would be like to see his mother again, but he discarded that thought as quickly as it came. James wasn't sure how far he should allow hope to grow.

The plan to take Zachary had backfired. It brought Amargat into the picture, and it was clear now that Zachary and Charlotte should be left alone. James wondered if Hugar had anything else up his sleeve. He didn't want to give up hope about his mother, if for no other reason than that Hugar had done so much for him.

He started walking back towards the cabin, but stopped before turning onto the footpath. He would wait and give Amos a little time alone. He couldn't help but feel that he was somehow intruding on personal ground.

He had been sitting there at the side of the road for about twenty minutes when someone walked around the bend. It was a woman with long, black hair flowing out from underneath a baseball cap, and she was coming downhill toward James. As she came closer, he saw that she wore olive green cargo pants and a khaki fleece vest. A brown backpack hung from her shoulders. She was looking downward, and most of her face was hidden under her cap.

When she was about fifteen yards away, James became slightly nauseated. His sight became unfocused. She would disappear for moments into the shadows of the trees. He stood as she approached. She kept her eyes on the ground and silently passed him. It was only when she turned onto the path to the cabin that he spoke.

"Rhiannon Alis?"

She paused, and it was several seconds before she turned to look at him. Her large eyes settled on him. At first, her eyes looked grey, or even white, but they flashed and seemed to darken to a bright blue. Her gaze held him there, and he waited.

"Why are you looking for Rhiannon Alis?"

"My friend is," he answered. His words felt fragile. He ventured a little more. "My friend, Amos."

No reaction. Her eyes stayed fixed on him. She had delicate features—a thin nose, ruby lips, and a little button chin. Her skin looked pale. Although it looked like she had been hiking, her complexion was clear and even with a slight azuline tint. Minutes went by, but James was relaxed. Strangely relaxed. Maybe Rhiannon Alis didn't want to be found. He would then be trespassing into her life. He understood this and hoped that somehow this was conveyed to her in the still silence. She stood there staring at him as if she was reading the pages of a book.

Suddenly, Amos ran out from the footpath.

"I thought I heard something," he blurted. He looked at the woman who calmly stood there. "Rhiannon Alis? I'm Amos Gillett. Son of Anne Gillett, nee Gyffes, who was the daughter of Ceridwyn Gyffes, nee Morgan." Even though Amos hadn't run very far, he was breathing heavily, his chest heaving as he waited for a response.

The woman looked at Amos pensively, tilting her head a bit.

"I'm sorry," she finally said. "It's been a while since I've had guests. Would you like to come into my home?"

Inside the small cabin, the woman served them tea. Amos was nearly ready to jump out of his skin, he was so excited. But she took her time, first boiling some water and putting the teapot out, then bringing out a tray of plates, tea cups and spoons. She had an assortment of teabags, so many that James couldn't make a choice.

She brought out a tin box, opened it, and carefully unwrapped some small cakes. They were shell-shaped. James popped a few into his mouth. They melted into his mouth, approximating very light and moist sponge cake. He tasted vanilla and lemon zest.

"These are great," James said, popping a few more into his mouth.

"They're called 'madeleines,'" she said. She smiled. "I hope they're still good. I made them over a week ago, before I went hiking."

Amos took a bite into one.

"Mmm, very fluffy," he said. "How do you keep them so soft for so long?"

"Oh, a woman has her secrets," she responded.

"We've all got our secrets, don't we, Jimmy?" asked Amos.

James shrugged while reaching for a few more madeleines.

Amos straightened up. "Here's mine," he said. "I'm descended from the God of the Horizon." He waited to see the woman's response.

She finished a sip of tea.

"Clever little title," she said. "What does the God of the Horizon do?"

This took Amos a little by surprise. "Um, I'm not sure."

"Is he a god of the sea?" she asked. "Does he take care of ships as they sail over the oceans?"

Amos had no response.

"Is he a god of the sky? Does he collect tolls from pilots who wander into his sky territories?"

The woman maintained her calm, serene voice.

"Or is he just some bloke who wanders around the earth getting women pregnant in the four corners?"

"I-I don't know," Amos stammered. "I was hoping you could tell me."

"I choose 'C,'" she said sweetly.

"Are you, or are you not, Rhiannon Alis Davies?" Amos said as he stood up.

"I am Shannon Morrison," she said. "I live here."

Amos sat down again. He implored, "Please, tell me the truth." Amos was not a man who cried often, but he was either on the verge of the greatest moment of his life, or the precipice of his deepest disappointment. The tears welled up in his eyes.

The woman looked surprised by his sudden emotion. Her jaw relaxed a bit. Then soon, tears also fell from her eyes.

"Yes, I was once Rhiannon Alis Rousseau. Before that, I was Rhiannon Alis Davies."

Amos walked over to where she was, and he hugged her.

"I've been searching for you for over fifteen years," he said. He held on for some time. Rhiannon's body relaxed, and her face lost its blue and gained some color.

"I see," Rhiannon said. "Thank you for not giving up."

That day, and in the days after, Rhiannon started to tell them parts of her story. Amos was more quiet than usual, happy, for once, to be just listening to another person talk. He had expected a story of glamor and adventure. But Rhiannon's story was not what he expected.

Chapter 15

Birds of a Feather

RHIANNON RECOUNTED parts of her story to Amos and James over the course of the next week. She would disappear for most of the morning, usually leaving the house before they had awoken. She would return and cook lunch for them, displaying a marvelous cooking ability. Lunch would be fairly quiet, as Rhiannon wasn't in much of a mood for talking after her morning excursions. After lunch, she worked in a small garden behind the cabin, or absconded again into the woods.

James fretted over whether he should call and update Hugar over the situation, but his loyalty was torn. He knew he needed to give Amos time. In addition, the cell phone Hugar had given James was dead. It was out of power, and James didn't know how to recharge it. No one had remembered to teach him how to do it. In any case, he was enjoying this quiet time in the San Gabriel Mountains and was not in a hurry to upset the situation.

Rhiannon did most of her sharing in the evening, after they had dinner. They would sit with hot chocolate or coffee, and she would tell her tale. Amos mostly listened. He was intent on listening and absorbing what she had to say. By the end of that first week, Rhiannon had described how she had run off to the Florida Keys, where she would spend the next forty years of her life. During those years, she spurned friendships, intentionally crafting an ill-boding aura that surrounded her. When necessary, she learned that she could scare the hell out of anyone who got in proximity to her by "squeezing" their brain and planting any number of dark thoughts. In that manner, she managed to be alone in all her time in the Keys.

"Jimmy here was chained up in the Mojave Desert for forty years," Amos said one evening. "The same amount of years you spent hidden away, in a sense."

Rhiannon looked at James with a strange smile. "Forty years in the desert," she said. "So you are ... like me?"

"We all are," Amos interjected. He then began to explain to her his long search, and how he had stumbled upon Hugar and others who were *special*. "Like you and I," he boasted.

"Special?" she asked, her eyes narrowing. "Do you know how much of a curse this has been? I'm over a hundred years old!" She stood up and extended her arms, looking at her skin. "What is this?" she repeated and pointed at her head. "What kind of freaks are we?"

"We're not freaks, Granny—"

She flashed another cold look, but after a moment, it was gone. Rhiannon laughed. "Granny, is it? I suppose I am."

"How come you never came back home?" asked Amos.

Rhiannon took a while to answer. "I had a new home," she said. "And it was my time to enjoy that new home."

"But Matthew died searching for you," Amos said, bluntly.

"I never asked anyone to come for me," she said.

Rhiannon then broke down in tears. "Ceridwyn wrote me to tell me about Matthew's death. She was so angry. I could read it in her writing. I did blame myself. I threw myself deeper and deeper into a black pit. What more do you want from me?"

"Well, did you know Ceridwyn killed herself after that?" asked Amos.

She drew a quick breath. Her shoulders slouched further. "I knew ... I knew she was gone. I felt it. But ... I didn't know how. To outlive your child, and even your grandchild, it is devastating,"

Amos tapped his foot restlessly against the ground.

"With all due respect, Granny, you left them. You left all of us. You could have had a lifetime with your daughter, your grandson. Maybe Ceri would still be alive if—"

Amos stopped talking, and his eyes glazed over. Rhiannon's face had gone frigid. Her skin turned to a slight tint of blue, and her eyes glared at Amos from an angle. Amos was imagining some great depth of sorrow. His gaze drifted off into the distance.

"Oh my God," he whispered. "No, no, no—what are you doing?" He looked at Rhiannon. "I'm so sorry, Granny. I'm sorry." He stood up abruptly and hurried out of the room.

James sat there alone with her. He shifted in his seat. A long while later, Rhiannon's face softened.

"He will never understand," she said.

James nodded to placate her.

"But you do, don't you, James? How time slows. Those of us who have this cursed blood perceive the passage of time differently. Years pass and nothing has changed. Our bodies firm, our eyes become brighter. We see others around us scramble and fight to use every minute of their youth before it dries up. Nothing is real or authentic unless they struggle for it in each and every moment. They don't know how to behold something from afar— to hold it at arm's length until a day in the unknown future when you can draw it near again and savor it. You sweeten your desires by denying them. I didn't fathom that they couldn't wait, my precious Ceri ... Matty. I didn't realize that they were less like my father, and more like my mother."

She stopped and looked at James. She blushed. "How terrible for you to have to witness our family spat. Enough of my ramblings. What of you? In these endless days of your youth, what do you yearn?"

Her eyes were searchlights into James's very soul. He squirmed in his chair. He wanted to shield his eyes from hers.

"I ... want to save my mother," he offered.

Her eyes dimmed for a moment, and her countenance took on sympathy, kindness.

"Of course, I understand. I would do anything, if I could somehow bring my mother back. Her name was Briallen Davies. We did not ... did not get along all too well, but there is so much I would like to share with her now. I understand her a little better after all this time. What was your mother like?"

"Her name was Emilia Worth. She was a schoolteacher at one time. I'm still ... remembering her."

"What do you mean?"

"I've forgotten ... many things. Different memories are still coming back. I hope to find her ... and complete the picture." James's face reddened. He felt like he was talking about things he didn't know. He diverted, "But what happened with your mother?"

Rhiannon thought for a while. "It is difficult for me, also, to access some of these far-flung memories. My mother was fairly happy when I was a child. We had each other, and she still had hope that my father would come back. But she lost the luster in her eyes over time, as it became more and more apparent that he was not coming back. I made due, but it was lonely sometimes in that house. By the time I was sixteen, I had met a boy and had my daughter Ceridwyn. Life moved on. Mama was loyal to a fault—always waited for my father. And she lost her youth doing so. She realized at some point that she was waiting for something that would never materialize.

"I watched her ... change, just like everyone else. Their bodies became weaker. Their minds became dimmer. They would chase love for some time, and then they would fall into these other categories that they had given themselves: elderly, grandfather, grandmother. They would become barren, first in the womb, then in the heart, and then the mind. I lived on and on and on, and in my years in the south of Florida, I tried to force myself into this same category. I waited to grow old and die. But, my body refuses to lose its vigor. My mind is still restless as ever. I still have the desires of youth. I still yearn."

She held her gaze steadily on James for a few moments. A voice crept into his consciousness. *Do you yearn?* It came like a thought, but it felt foreign. *Had she said something?* He noticed her lips. They glistened, and they quivered gently. He looked at the soft line of jaw. He traced it from her chin to where it almost met her left ear. James felt a slight panic. His face became warm. There was a stirring in his body and urgency in his breath. He stood up abruptly. They locked eyes. The walls of the cabin swayed, and the lights from a chandelier swung around him.

"Good night," he said softly, and he left the room.

Rhiannon let out a soft sigh, and she leaned back into her chair to rest.

The next day, Amos asked James for some time alone with Rhiannon. Amos wanted to apologize to his great-great-grandmother and needed privacy. James left the cabin in the mid-morning, before Rhiannon had returned from her morning trek. For a few hours, he hiked through the woods, not on any trail, but stomping and climbing along the mountainside. He needed to do this more, he decided. The physical activity energized him, and he rejoiced in being able to move under the shadows of the treetops, breathing in the fresh mountain air.

The further he went, instead of getting tired, he felt stronger. He put the complications of human relationships behind him and sprinted among the trees. He climbed and leapt and swung from branches. He was soon springing from tree to tree, exhilarated by the growing power in his torso and in his limbs. He was smashing into tree trunks, crashing into the forest floor, barreling down the mountainside. Before long, mud smeared his face and arms, and his

T-shirt was nearly ripped in half. His jeans were in tatters. But he felt alive. He had shrugged off the worries of the day.

He walked back to the cabin, smiling, as the sun started its daily journey toward the western horizon. When he arrived at the cabin, the others were settling in for dinner. They were sitting at the table when James came in, and Rhiannon immediately burst into laughter.

"What in the world happened to you?" asked Amos.

"You're just a great big ape, aren't you?" Rhiannon said. She ran over and fussed over him, checking his arms and face for cuts or other injuries but laughing the whole while.

"Just got a little carried away, running around," James said.

"Amos, this won't do, you're going to have to go pick up some new clothes for him," she said.

"Me?" he protested. "Why can't he go and get it himself?"

"Look at him," she said. "I know this is the only clothes he's got. It's all he's been wearing for over a week. Shame on you for not getting him some more clothes."

"But I'm hungry," Amos whined.

"Fine, after dinner then," she said. "But then you're going to have to go into the city to find anything open."

They ate a quiet dinner. Amos fumed just a little bit, looking over at mud-splattered James a couple of times and shaking his head. Rhiannon gave him directions to a store back down the mountain and gave him some money. "Get three or four outfits for him before you come back," she yelled as he plodded away from the cabin.

"And you, I don't have anything your size, so go wash up and wrap yourself in this blanket until Amos gets back," she ordered.

James did as he was told, going to the bathroom to take a shower.

He came out with the old maroon blanket wrapped around his waist.

"I put a fire on. Keep yourself warm until Amos comes back." She brought him a tray of madeleines and hot chocolate.

"Thank you," James said.

She stood there after putting the tray down next to where James sat.

"Well, are you going to invite me to sit down?"

"Um, please sit," James said.

"I may be just an old woman, but I like some chivalry every once in a while," she said.

"You're not an old woman."

"I'm a hundred nineteen years old."

"You don't look it."

They sat in silence for a few minutes. Rhiannon turned and leaned towards him.

"You've got a lot going in your head for someone so quiet," she said.

"I'm not thinking of nothing."

"Oh, you are. It's as loud as a railroad station in here."

"What am I thinking about then?"

"You were thinking about how you were jumping from tree to tree earlier," she said. "How amazing to be able to do that."

"It was fun," he smiled.

"Then you were thinking about your walk home, thinking about how the heck you were going to find your mother."

"I don't have a clue."

"And then you were thinking about me," she whispered. "Thinking about my eyes."

"Was I?" James asked. He leaned away on his chair and looked to the other side of the room.

"Look over here," she said.

He turned his gaze back at her. She was right. He had been thinking about how he could see the fire reflected in her eyes. They were like mirrors of their surroundings. He could spot himself in their reflection. They were gorgeous eyes, but where was she? He wondered if he could see her soul within them, but he only saw himself and the flickering of firelight. He looked at her flawless skin, once again tracing the lines of her face. He couldn't remember if he had ever touched a woman.

"Go ahead," she said. "Touch me."

He slowly reached out a hand. Rhiannon closed her eyes, and his fingers finally lighted upon her cheek. He stroked it gently, afraid his calloused fingers would hurt her. He caressed the line of her jaw, from her ear to her chin. She quivered.

"Tell me," she said. "Say it, please."

"You're not a freak at all," he said, his voice suddenly strong and clear. "You're beautiful." He fought back a great urge to embrace her.

She exhaled. Her shoulders collapsed. She looked up again, and tears were streaming down her face.

"I'm sorry," she said. "I know you're not him. It's not your job."

"Who?" James asked.

"Never mind," she said. "Oh, look at me." She sat up straight and wiped the tears from her face. She smiled at him. "I'm glad you're here. You and Amos. It's good to feel connected again. It's good to feel alive again."

"If there's anything I can do—"

"Just talk to me," she said. "Don't leave too quickly. Spying on people's thoughts is the loneliest pastime in the world. I'm enjoying hearing someone's voice again. Someone safe."

James did his best, asking the questions that came to his mind. He tried to elaborate on the answers that he gave to her questions, instead of just muttering yes or no. He was glad to look into her glass-and-ice eyes, filled with the firelight, and thinking that somewhere behind that veneer, he was warming her heart too.

He told her the stories about Borus and Margaret. He shared about Zachary, Charlotte, and the inimitable Amargat. She reacted with awe and bewilderment, and he managed not to wonder whether she had already plumbed the depths of his mind for these nuggets of his past.

"Why do you think we're like this, James?" Rhiannon looked at him expectantly. He hesitated. He felt like he had no wisdom to offer. But she continued to wait for his answer with those impenetrable eyes. He thought about it. He thought about his own years in purgatory. He had seen for himself through a pain and emptiness that seemed eternal that something good could still happen. He saw that purpose could still return and fill his life.

"I think it's never over," he said. "I think life could still offer a few surprises."

"So after all these years of loneliness and angst," she replied, "you think it's possible to still have joy?"

"Yeah, I guess I do."

They talked as the fire started to die out. They talked until Amos came home, grouchy and complaining that Rhiannon hadn't given him the right directions to the store. He had gotten lost. But James and Rhiannon went to bed grateful that, somehow, destiny had surprises yet in store. For them, forty years was not such a long time anymore, and at least for today, they were not alone.

Chapter 16

A Goddess Who Is Half Nymph

AMOS GREW SULLEN and restless. He was less and less willing with every passing day to stay in that cabin in the mountains. He was particularly ill at ease one day as they were having lunch behind the cabin. The sun was shining from a clear blue sky, yet Amos was fidgety.

"I've got a confession to make," he suddenly said.

Rhiannon had begun the practice of staying out of both of their thoughts. Amos had insisted she stopped "snooping" around in his mind. She had also come to believe that it was best, out of respect for Amos, James, and any other person she met, to not do so unless absolutely necessary. The temptation to search Amos's mind was only fleeting, and she quickly resisted.

"I've been in contact with Charlotte again," Amos said.

"What for?" James asked, looking up from his meatloaf.

"Well, I had been thinking," Amos continued, "that I really did skip out on you and Hugar, what with the mission to find your mum. So I contacted her about it."

"And?" Rhiannon asked. Waiting for people to speak out their thoughts was a patience-testing exercise for her.

"And she is going to come and give us some information," Amos said.

"What do you mean she's going to come?" asked Rhiannon, putting down her fork and knife. "You invited her here?"

"She already knew about this place," he said. "That's why I even knew how to find you."

"Yes, but you didn't have to invite her back! Why didn't you arrange to meet her somewhere else?"

"I don't know!" yelped Amos. "I just text messaged her and asked if she could help, and she responded with a short message that she and Zachary would be come by."

"She and Zachary?" asked James. "You know he's got to be seething about what I did to him!"

"Oh, Amos!" yelled Rhiannon. "When are they supposed to be here?"

Amos looked at his cell phone. "Well, they're actually already five minutes late."

It was then that a great hissing sound came from above. The sun was suddenly blotted out. The three of them looked up to see two pairs of impressive wings, spanning ten feet each, descending upon them. The winged creatures exploded in smoke. Moments later, hands grabbed James, and he was thrown from the table.

As James picked himself up, he caught a glimpse of Zachary, dressed in black as always, lunging at him. They collided, both men rolling through the dirt. Zachary, screaming, pummeled James as they tumbled.

"Oh, sweet Mary!" Amos shouted as he jumped up from his seat. Smoke gathered and swirled before him, and Charlotte took shape before his eyes.

"Now, now, Amos," she said. "Give them some time to work out their differences."

"You're supposed to be here to help," Amos said, and he tried to brush by Charlotte.

She grabbed him by the arm, pulling him close to her.

"You're quite strong," Amos squeaked. His voice trembled as he looked aghast at her.

Zachary and James had both gotten to their feet. Tossing aside tactics, they both launched mighty blows, landing punch after punch. James knocked his foe back considerably with each hit, but Zachary was fast, moving all around James and landing two or three blows at a time.

Rhiannon, who had frozen in her chair for the first few hectic moments, stood up. She balled her hands into tight fists, pursed her lips, and then focused on Zachary. A high-pitch sound cut into Zachary's brain. He stopped in mid-punch, holding his hands to his ears. It was no use. The piercing noise drilled into his mind.

"What are you doing to him!" Charlotte screamed. She let go of Amos and leapt over the table towards Rhiannon.

A wide shadow was cast across the grassy opening. Something crashed into the earth, sending reverberations that knocked all five of them to the ground. The mountainside trembled as they looked to the source.

"Wow," said Rhiannon, fear in her eyes. She scampered on the ground backwards, joining Amos.

If the twins' wings had spanned ten feet each, the figure before them stood twelve feet tall with wings that stretched out to over twenty feet. It stood silhouetted by the sun, a low rumbling coming from its throat.

Charlotte pulled herself off the ground and stood facing the great winged creature.

"We told you we would handle it, Father!" she complained.

"YOU PLAY CHILDREN'S GAMES."

"It was Zachary's fault," Charlotte said, "as always."

"Shut up, sister!" Zachary cried out. "She was riling me up the entire flight over here, telling me how James Henry had beat me up."

"No one should ever be blamed for telling the truth," she responded.

The massive figure exploded in a storm of black smoke. As the air cleared, Amargat walked forward. "Enough," he said. "I had already told James that all accounts between us were settled. You made me into a liar."

"Sorry, Father," the twins said together.

James, slightly bloodied, walked up to Amargat.

"Hello again, sir," he said.

Amargat reached out a lanky arm and shook James's hand.

"I'm awfully sorry, James," he said. He looked around at the others, and the table with food. "And we even interrupted a meal. Please forgive my children and I for this inconvenience."

"No problem," James said.

Nodding his head toward Amos and Rhiannon, Amargat asked, "Ahem, would you do the honor of introductions?"

"Oh yes, of course. The man there is Amos Gillett, and the girl is Rhiannon Alis, um—"

"Rousseau," Rhiannon said. She walked forward slowly. Approaching Amargat, she gave a meek smile and extended a trembling hand.

Amargat crossed his left foot behind his right, took her hand, and then bowed to kiss it.

"It is a pleasure to meet you, my lady," he said.

She curtsied in reply and then looked at James, who nodded at her and mouthed, "It's okay."

Amos tiptoed to Rhiannon's side and said, "Hello again, Mr. Blackbyrd."

Amargat chuckled. "Good day, Amos! I wasn't aware that people still used that nickname. Please, if you must use a surname, call me Abkhazi."

"Certainly, whatever is best, Mr. Abkhazi."

"So, I believe we are here to assist with a matter," Amargat said.

"That's right," said Amos. "I had contacted Charlotte for help in finding James's mother."

Amargat looked at James.

"My mother disappeared around the same time I was imprisoned in the desert," James said. "I'm hoping that she might still be alive, somewhere."

"Charlotte, I believe you know something about this," Amargat said.

"Yes, I was about to get to it, Father, when you arrived," Charlotte said. She walked into the middle of the group and posed with her head tilted back and a hand in the air. "A goddess who is half a nymph with glancing eyes and fair cheeks and half again a huge snake, great and awful, with speckled skin, eating raw flesh beneath the secret parts of the holy earth. She keeps guard—a nymph who dies not nor grows old all her days." She paused and looked at James. "Does that sound familiar?"

He closed his eyes and thought back in time.

"Long ago, I had a dream about a woman who was also a snake," James said. "I dreamt that I was her prisoner, but I broke free, struck her, and ran."

"Yes, you killed her, you brute," Charlotte said, putting a hand to her forehead with mock distress. "Echidna is dead in a tomb, in the same place you encountered her."

"What does this have to do with my mother?"

"Do you remember a gem or stone, embedded in the nymph's head?" Amargat asked.

James reached again into his memory, and it became clear.

"There was a great big gemstone," he said. "It thrust out of her head from between her eyes to the top of her forehead."

"As you know, James," Amargat said, "gems and stones can be imbued with special qualities. Using old sorcery, that frankly, I wouldn't dare touch, one can even turn the appropriate gem into a prison."

"Prison?" Rhiannon jumped in. "You mean James's mother is in that gemstone?"

"That is what one could suspect."

"Well," Amos said. "Echidna is the nymph who keeps *guard.*"

"I woke up in her prison cell," James said. "I escaped, but I suppose she was my jailer."

"And it is quite possible that you weren't the only she was guarding," Amos said.

"James, you've got to find out," Rhiannon said. "Don't you?"

He nodded. He saw that great red stone in his mind.

"I don't remember where Echidna's lair was," he said.

"Charlotte can tell you," Amargat offered. "But mind you, we cannot go with you on this venture. In the end, this is your affair that you must handle."

"Of course," James said. "I understand."

"We can't let James go alone," Rhiannon said, turning to Amos. "We have to go with him."

"It's likely to be very dangerous," Amos said.

Charlotte sauntered over to Amos. Pulling out a piece of paper, she whispered into his ear. He jerked away quickly.

"I'm giving you directions, silly boy," she said, leaning in again.

Amargat walked up close to James and wrapped a long arm around him.

"Listen," he whispered. "I know the woman behind all this, Margaret. She was my dear wife's sister. As I think you know, she was also married to your father. She and your father were supposed to be the new royal couple, the shining heralds of a new era for those of us few Watchers who remain. They would beget a new army of children. Heh. Except, she was barren. That is why she did what she did to you, and your mother. That is why she stole my children, once they were born. She is a bitter, desperate adversary, James. I understand you biding your time in this mountain … retreat. But you must realize you are in a new game, now, don't you? It's not enough to be a man. You must be more than that."

Amargat gave James a small nod of the head, pat on his back, and turned to the others. Charlotte was finishing up with Amos. She had given him some notes and a map. Amargat gestured to her and Zachary, and they came to him.

"If you will excuse us, dear friends," Amargat said, "we'll leave you to your discourse. May you find favor on your quest."

"Good-bye," said James, "and thank you."

With another bow, and then explosions of smoke, they were in their winged forms. Amargat and his children flew into the sky, the beating of their vast wings aggravating a storm of dirt and leaves.

James turned to Rhiannon. "You two shouldn't come, especially not you, Rhiannon," he said.

"Oh shush. We're coming with you!" she said. "I'm not going to leave you alone with this."

Amos furrowed his brow and bowed his head.

"We don't know what we're going to find in that tomb," Amos said. "I think we have to get Hugar and Quetzal up there too."

"Sure, do that," James said.

"We'll start tomorrow," Amos said. He looked at the notes Charlotte gave him. "It's in the middle of nowhere in northern Cali. Sounds like it's going to take a couple of days."

The next morning, they got some supplies together and piled into the car. The trio then caught the 210 Freeway, heading northwest for about twenty miles until they transitioned onto the 5 Freeway.

Amos's mood lightened considerably once they were on the road again. He was behind the wheel, and he began to impart upon them his knowledge of the Interstate 5.

"It's the only interstate highway to touch both the US-Canadian border and the US-Mexican border," he explained. "I've driven the entire way."

"Wow, Amos," said Rhiannon. "It's a bit like me driving from New York City to Key West back in 1953."

"Exactly, Granny," he beamed. "We are family, after all. Free spirits!"

They drove over the Tehachapi Mountains, coming down along the stretch called the Grapevine, named after the canyon that the freeway ran along. In front of them, a huge expanse of flat land, the San Joaquin Valley, spread out before them. The San Joaquin Valley was part of the greater Central Valley, Amos explained, which would extend for about 450 miles north/northwest through California, covering over 22,000 square miles.

It was a bromidic journey through dull and depressed rural country that was nevertheless productive agricultural land. Much of this part of the valley was semi-arid desert, and the farmland was watered through irrigation or from underground wells.

Rhiannon sat in the front seat with Amos, and James was soon napping in the back seat. The hot, flat land reminded him of the Mojave Desert, and he found the monotony of this part of the journey oppressive.

After about five hours, they passed through the state capital, Sacramento, and the land grew greener and more lush. Here, the valley was called the Sacramento Valley, and they were approaching the mountains and great national forests of Northern California.

By that evening, they decided to stop in Redding, a city at the northern edge of the great valley. They had traversed the entire Central Valley of California, and they would rest for the night. From the west, north, and east of the city, the Cascade Range loomed before them. This was one of the great mountain ranges in the west of North America, extending from the region around Redding through Oregon, Washington, and then into Canada.

They were going to enter its heights and attempt to find Echidna's corpse and her great gemstone. James went to sleep hoping that his mother's soul still throbbed from within, in the red light of the gem.

They drove east from Redding, taking the 299 Highway. Very quickly, they went from the valley floor into the Cascade foothills, then rose into the Klamath Mountains. The many species of fir, pine, and spruce trees swiftly surrounded them, rising along the curving highway. The 299 Highway would wind and meander eastward through the mountains and forests of northern California, curling for part of its journey along the Trinity River, then sweeping through the grand redwood trees near the coast before ending at the Pacific Ocean. It was a resplendent drive through stunning scenery. But they would not be going so far.

"We're heading into the Trinity Alps Wilderness," Amos explained.

The Trinity Alps Wilderness was a vast area northwest of Redding, covering more than 500,000 acres. It was a land of secluded lakes, high and jagged granite peaks, black bears, wolverines, and some of the highest concentration of conifers in the world. Unlike some of the other wilderness areas and national parks in northern California, the Trinity Alps Wilderness was seldom visited and lightly traveled. In its isolated back country, adventurers reported Bigfoot sightings more often than anywhere else in the Pacific Northwest. In order to find Echidna's tomb, they would be entering remote land.

As the highway twisted through the mountains, they passed ghost towns, old mining whistle-stops that had since lost their pulses. Occasionally, houses dotted the mountainside off the highway, inhabited by brave souls who savored their cloistered, hermetic lifestyles. After ninety miles, they turned off the highway onto Denny Road, wriggling northward. It had been nearly three hours since they left Redding when they turned onto a dirt road. It was blocked by an old abandoned gate. James got out of the car and forced the gate off its rusted hinges. He tossed the gate aside, and they continued, snaking ever slower into the backcountry.

The dirt road became narrow and overgrown. James had to repeatedly exit the car to clear away brush. Rhiannon took over at the wheel, while Amos poured over his notes and map and navigated. They were using old trails used long ago by miners, and their sedan shook and rumbled over the terrain. They knew they could not drive much further. Amos decided they would stop the car where the trail converged with a river and entered a heavily forested area. He estimated that it would take a further seven hours on foot to reach their destination.

They grabbed their supplies and trekked into the shadows of the trees. Rhiannon insisted on looking at Amos's notes, and then she started taking the lead. This agitated him, but Rhiannon made good time. She was sure-footed and comfortable, even as the terrain became more and more rugged. She drifted through the trees and up the rising slope of the land like a forest sprite.

"We need to cross the river," Amos announced.

"The current's pretty strong," Rhiannon replied. She looked at James. "But maybe that's not too big of a problem today."

They entered the water in between two bends in the river. They were in a line parallel to the current, standing side by side and holding each other's backpack straps and clothing. James marched in at the upstream position. The strong water didn't budge him as his boots dug heavily into the mud and rocks of the river bed. Rhiannon and Amos stayed on his downstream side, sheltered from the bulk of the current's wrath. The three made it to the other side with no incident.

"You're pretty useful to have around on these hikes," laughed Rhiannon. She punched James in the shoulder and then yelped in mock pain.

"Let's carry on," Amos said. "No time for fun and games."

James's thoughts were turning more and more to Echidna's lair. He wondered if his mother was really there. He wondered if Echidna was really dead. A creeping angst began to shadow him as he hiked closer and closer to the reality that waited.

They turned away from the river to follow a small creek. The trail was rising higher and higher. The slope narrowed, the lands falling away from them on either side, and James could see that they were climbing towards a jagged ridgeline that now dominated their view toward the east. He kept an eye on Rhiannon, but she was scaling the rugged terrain easily, setting an aggressive pace for them. Amos, meanwhile, was slowing down and falling behind them.

As they clawed up along segments of the rocky ridge, they discovered blackened slopes. Dark smoke hovered like an army of ghosts above the charred chaparral.

"Must have been a fire this past summer," Rhiannon said.

She marched forward, but Amos hung back, looking spooked by the suddenly ominous vista. James also felt a fear creeping up his spine. An ever so subtle queasiness sinuated through his body.

"Com'on, boys!" Rhiannon yelled from up the ridge. She was unaffected.

James shook himself out of his stupor and walked back to Amos. He took Amos's backpack and patted him on the back.

"Let's go, buddy," James said.

He helped Amos scale the remaining steep portions of the climb up the canyon, lifting him up onto ledges and generally dragging him along some of the steep inclines. They climbed past ancient rocks, striated from the slow passage of prehistoric glaciers. The dread and disquietude remained, but James used it to motivate himself, and he quickened his own pace while exhorting and pushing Amos along.

Eventually, they made it to the ridgeline. Around them, the peaks and mountains undulated in lines as far as the eye could see.

Rhiannon shouted in joy.

"So you say my father is the God of the Horizon?" she asked Amos. "Well, then this must be his courtyard."

Amos was sore and tired, and he barely grunted in reply. He didn't look at Rhiannon or James in the eyes, trudging slowly forward while mostly looking at the ground. If anything, Rhiannon's enthusiasm chaffed at him.

They pushed along the ridgeline for several more miles, hiking past a pristine lake below them in the shadowed eastern slope. The ridgeline extended southward, and as the sun sank toward the horizon to their right, a dark peak began to tower in the distance.

"Wait," muttered Amos. "It's close."

He collapsed to the ground, kneeling. Whereas James and Rhiannon had endured the trek well, Amos looked beaten. His lips were chapped, his eyes unfocused. Rhiannon came and knelt beside him, offering him water. He drank sloppily, water spilling onto the front of his shirt.

"I can't do it," he said. "I can't go further."

"We can wait here, Amos," Rhiannon said. "We'll rest."

"No, no, no." He shook his head.

"We have supplies," she said. "We can even camp here for the evening and continue in the morning."

"No, I can't do that," Amos said. He hung his head as he sat on the ground, elbows resting on his knees. "I called Hugar. I sent him the instructions on how to get here and when to meet James. He and Quetzal will be here within a few hours. They will have to travel the same path we took."

"And you don't want to be here when they get here?" Rhiannon asked.

"No, I don't."

James stepped forward.

"I don't think Hugar's going to hold anything against you," James said, "for what you did."

"Then you don't know Hugar too well, do you?" snapped Amos. "Don't you get it? I'm nothing to him. I'm just another piece of crap human. And look at me, I'm pathetic. Can't even keep myself together." He looked up at James. "Look at you! You're not even breaking a sweat. What am I even doing here? This has nothing to do with me anymore."

He stood up and turned to Rhiannon.

"Amos, what's wrong?" she asked.

"I'm done," he said. "I've done my part. Let the hero here do his part." He finally made eye contact with Rhiannon. "Are you coming with me, or are you staying?"

She hesitated. Amos walked over to her and placed his hands on her shoulders.

"Listen," Amos said. "We're family. Jimmy, he's gonna be all right. He's got his own family coming."

Rhiannon looked into Amos's eyes and saw that he was resolute. She contemplated the ridge ahead of them, and the southern dark peak in the distance. Something hostile seemed to growl from the south. Even Rhiannon lost some courage at that moment. She nodded softly.

"Good," Amos said. He turned to James. "All you need to know is on my notes here. You want to find the ravine below on the western slope. Follow the ravine southward. It cuts down toward the base of that peak, and there you'll find an old mine. That's where you want to go."

"Thanks," James said.

Rhiannon walked over to James.

"I'm sorry," she said. "I wanted to help. You ... you take care down there."

"I understand," James said. "Amos is right. You take care of yourself too."

The two of them picked up their packs and turned back to the north. Rhiannon looked back once at James, but then the two of them were gone over a rise. James perused the notes that Amos had given him. He turned back towards the peak that loomed in the south. Walking along the edge of the ridge, he surveyed the western slope. After another ten minutes, he spotted a ravine below. The slope was steep, with very little vegetation. He scanned the area and chose a segment that he thought he might be able to climb down.

He was halfway down to the ravine when his foothold crumbled. Flailing his arms, he was unable to find anything to grasp. He fell backwards. He was airborne for a few seconds before he smashed into the side of the mountain. He saw a blur of the red rock wall, and streaks of blue sky as he tumbled head over heels.

He careened into the ravine, breaking through a net of dry branches before finally crashing into the ground. Even with his remarkable constitution, James blacked out as pain coursed throughout his body.

Chapter 17

The Demons of the Ravine

HIS VISION SLOWLY coalesced. The blackness retreated and spindly arms and fingers appeared, hovering above him. They were branches hanging overhead, gently swaying in the breeze. He was lying on his back. The sky that he saw through the tree tops was darkening. As his consciousness returned, he became aware of pockets of pain that stilled throbbed in his body. Severe agony screamed at him from the fingers on his left hand, and he brought the hand to his face. Several of the fingers were mangled grotesquely—the skin was black and blue. He looked at his right hand, confirming that it still functioned. With his right hand, he twisted the fingers on his left back into place.

He sat up, and his head spun. His body convulsed and his blood vessels and nerve endings pulsated. His body was still suffering, but healing. His left hand began to regain some of its color, and he felt the sensation of a thousand needles entering his palm. As he was able to move both hands again, he then sensed the pulsating ache in his jaw. He placed his hands at the sides of his face, and felt his jaw protruding far to the right. He snapped it back into place, and then screamed in pain.

James stood up slowly, stumbling as his equilibrium continued to seesaw. His vision dimmed, his surroundings fading away as he took a step, and his brain felt like it was thrashing itself against his skull. He stumbled forward.

With the sun nearing its plunge below the western horizon, the ravine was enveloped in darkness. As he crept along, the sounds of wildlife echoed through the gulch. The shrieks of birds and the scampering of beasts in the underbrush rattled from ear to ear, and they sounded like hastening demons shadowing him from his sides and overhead in the jagged canopy. He dragged onward, trying to quicken his pace and calm his mind. Plunging into the murky lair of Echidna would be preferable to staying out in the maddening ravine.

He sensed that the serrated edges of the ravine overhead were the fanged jaws of a great demon, awakening itself from the earth's crust, ready to swallow him alive into another long nightmare. His head throbbed, and he thought he heard howls and cries from behind him. He hurried forward, his extraordinary strength of no use to him in the mouth of a devil. As he rushed forward, the dark branches of the surrounding trees seemed to reach for him. Their shadows clawed at him from all sides, and their whispers taunted him. *It's too late for you. It's too late for your mother.*

The demons of the ravine were now gathered behind him, giving chase, calling his name. He lost his sense for which way was forward. The shadow-claws clutched at him and the dark ravine spiraled around him. He fell to the ground.

Turning upon his back, he faced his pursuers. The white-bluish eyes of the devil of the ravine emerged. It had come from the depths of the earth to take him at last. He heard his name called. They were calling him to submit himself into the darkness. He closed his eyes and gave himself.

James lost consciousness for only a few moments. His heels dragged on the ground. He was held by both arms—it sounded like a man on each side of him, breathing heavily. James dug a heel into the ground and propelled himself upwards while shrugging off the grips of his two captors.

He spun around to face them.

"Oh thank goodness, you big jerk."

The voice was familiar, but James was blinded by two bright lights.

"James, it's us." Another man's voice.

The two men came a little closer and raised the lights to their faces.

"What's gotten into you, man?" It was Quetzal.

Hugar stood next to him.

"Are you alright?" asked Hugar. "We approached you earlier, but you ran like a madman."

"Hey, let's just find this mine, quick," said Quetzal. "This place gives me the creeps."

"And you think Echidna's tomb is going to be any more hospitable?" asked Hugar.

"Sorry, guys," mumbled James. "I'm a little disoriented."

The three of them forged onward. James didn't feel quite so dizzy any longer. The fear still slithered up his back like snakes, but he was encouraged now that Quetzal and Hugar were by his side. His backpack was gone, but the other two had some supplies, in addition to the two bright lamps.

"What happened to you, anyway?" asked Quetzal.

"I fell, trying to climb down from the ridge," answered James. "How did you two get down?"

"We didn't follow Charlotte's path," said Hugar. "Amos—sometimes you have to tell him exactly what to do if you want things done right. The directions Charlotte gave you were from her point of view—a view from the sky that is. I extrapolated exactly where this mine is based on the information and devised another route. It still took quite a bit of climbing, but at least we didn't have to scale that ridge just to have to make a dangerous descent into the ravine. Where is that fool, anyhow? Skip out again?"

"He decided he'd had enough," James said.

"That figures," Hugar said. "You should have called me as soon as you found him. I've been losing my mind trying to call you for weeks."

"Sorry, I don't know how to power my phone."

Quetzal laughed. "Everything we've been teaching you, and no one remembered to teach you how to charge your phone."

"And how did you manage to find our friend, Mr. Gillett?" asked Hugar.

James had to think back.

"You sent me to the twins' house in Las Vegas."

"Yes, that's right. That was the last I heard from you."

"I found an address on some postcards. I went there and met Amargat again."

"You met the Blackbyrd again?" asked Quetzal. "How many times are you going to survive encounters with that badass?"

"I don't know," said James. "He was nice ... that second time."

"And he led you to Mr. Gillett?" asked Hugar.

"Yes, he gave me this stone, and the stone ... told me where Amos was."

"Hmm, sounds like a—how would you call it in English—a memory stone," said Hugar.

"How many of these Watchers, like Amargat and Father, are there in the world?" asked James. "What are they doing here?"

"That is a good question, my brother," said Hugar. "I don't know a whole lot myself. But you deserve to know more than you do. Let's make a deal. We'll get out of this ravine alive first. Then I shall tell you everything."

They plodded along the pitch-black gulch for another half an hour. Finally, they reached the end of it. At first, they thought it was a dead end. The peak that James had seen earlier that day from the ridge towered over them, just a monstrous silhouette obstructing the stars of the sky. They searched about with their lamps, and it was Quetzal who found an opening in the mountainside, covered by overgrown brush. Tearing the vegetation aside, he cast his light into the opening. A tunnel, covered in cobwebs, led further into the earth.

"You're right, this doesn't look any better than out here in the ravine," he said.

Quetzal hesitantly led them into the tunnel. It continued for about a hundred yards at a gentle decline before opening up into a larger area. Hugar and Quetzal walked around, shining their lamps. The area they were in connected to several separate rooms that had been built into the larger cavern. James walked over to an area on the left. Rusted bars cordoned off a small cell.

"Over here," Quetzal called.

In an adjacent space, an old rotted table stood. On top of the long table was a crate.

"Looks like old rusted tools and blades," said Quetzal.

"I've been here before," said James.

"You've been here, in this room?" asked Hugar.

"Long ago, before my time in the desert, I woke up in that cell in the next room. Echidna came and led me to this room."

"What happened?" asked Hugar.

"She was going to cut me with one of these rusted blades, and I struck her and ran. I don't remember much after that."

"So Mr. Gillett was telling me the truth over the phone," said Hugar.

"Let's find this Echidna," said Quetzal, "if it's really down here."

"Stay close together," added Hugar.

They moved about more boldly, energized by the expectation that Echidna's gem waited for them somewhere in the mine. They discovered more rooms, probably old office or storage space, but it was clear that the mine had been out of use for a very long time. They stayed together, combing through the various tunnels. Some of the tunnels looped back into one of the main caverns. It was not that big of a mine, and before long, they had been through every room and tunnel.

"It's time to split up," Hugar said. "This time, pay special attention to the walls and floors."

With only two lamps, James went with Quetzal. The two of them went back to the first cavern. They took care to examine the walls. James strayed from the light, feeling about in the dark and tapping his foot on the ground to check for trap doors. After some time, they heard Hugar's voice from deeper in the mine.

"Come here," he called. "Down the long tunnel."

Hugar was at the end of the central tunnel that went deepest into the mountain. He was kneeling on the ground, wiping a section of soil away. He pounded twice on the ground. The sound was wooden and hollow. James and Quetzal joined him, and all three of them knelt to clear away the dirt. They discovered a large, heavy wooden door buried under the thin layer of soil. They found neither knob nor handle to be able to open the door. Hugar nodded at James, who stood over the door in the ground and brought down his boot. After a few stomps, the door had been shattered. They ripped the remaining sections off of the rusted hinges and cleared the entrance way.

Quetzal lowered his lamp and looked down below. He shrugged and jumped right on it. James followed. Hugar noticed that there was a wooden ladder and climbed down. They were in another tunnel. It continued at a decline another thirty yards before opening up into a large cavern. This cavern was larger than any of the previous ones in the mine. It was already about fifteen yards wide and becoming wider as they walked forward. Soon, they couldn't see the cavern walls to either side. The three continued close together down the center of the cavern.

"It's thick here," said Hugar, "that sickening mixture of nausea and fear that we've felt since entering the ravine. It emanates from here."

In the spacious cavern, the light of their lamps didn't go very far, but in the distance in front of them, something was coming into view. They slowed their pace and approached with lamps raised. It was an immense sculpture. The light brought the object out of the darkness. James cringed as he saw its features—the large, foreboding nostrils set over the snarling jaws; the horns twisting outward and forward from the head, ending in two sharp points; the undulating sinews of muscle captured in bronze.

"Oh my," Hugar said.

It was a statue of Borus, enshrined in dark bronze. It crouched in mid-roar and was set upon a shoulder-high pedestal of stone. They inched closer. The bronze-working was impeccable. The three stood in awe, looking up at the intimidating figure.

After a while, Hugar cast his light further into the cavern.

"There," he said, "the cavern ends."

Quetzal went further, not more than twenty-five feet, and he found the far wall.

"Looks like something is here," he said. "Looks like someone tied together branches into a make-shift door."

James joined him. Twigs had been tied together by twine, and they covered something hidden within the cavern wall.

"Something's behind here," Quetzal said, lifting his lamp and peering between the branches.

Suddenly, they heard Hugar cry behind them. Turning around, they saw Hugar being lifted by the neck. He was flung into the darkness of the cavern. They heard Hugar scream once more as he crashed to the ground. His lamp flew along with him into the darkness, and then it was extinguished.

The statue of Borus was coming alive.

Quetzal and James ran to the right, giving a wide berth to Borus. They searched for Hugar with the lone lamp they had remaining.

"There he is," James shouted.

Hugar had been thrown a great distance. He was bloodied, but already trying to stand.

"Are you alright?" Quetzal asked.

"Don't worry about me," he replied. "Let's focus on this blasted abomination." They stood together, but the lamp didn't cast light very far.

"Listen for him," Quetzal whispered.

They heard a great boom as Borus leapt down from his pedestal. Then it roared. The three men crept backwards as Borus's horrendous scent reached them and buckled their knees. The ground trembled as Borus stampeded toward the trio.

"Get out of the way!" Hugar yelled.

Quetzal leapt to the right. James, frozen, stared into the darkness. In the faint light of the lone lamp, the ivory horns and spikes of Borus appeared. Hugar yelled something and then pulled at James with all his might. The two men tumbled to the left as Borus stormed through the area they had just been.

Hugar grabbed for James's face in the dark.

"Get up! Get up and fight!" he yelled.

James stood up, but he was in total darkness. He saw Quetzal's light across the cavern. He ran towards it. All three men converged again, huddling in the small sphere of light. They listened for Borus.

"How well can he see in the dark?" asked Quetzal.

"If he can't see us, you can rest assured that he can smell us," said Hugar.

"Then that means we're sitting ducks cowering together like this," said Quetzal. "Here you take this."

He gave his lamp to James.

"We'll even the odds," he said.

Quetzal slipped into the blackness surrounding them. As he did, his body began to change. It contracted, his posture stooped over, his skin darkened. For a moment, James and Hugar could see bright yellow eyes gleaming.

"That is his second form," whispered Hugar.

"Like Zachary and Charlotte," said James.

"Yes."

"And you?"

"No, I have only this one form," said Hugar. "Like you, brother."

They heard another roar in the distance, this time it was the cry of a great cat, followed by deep-throated growling. They ran towards the ruckus. As they neared, the faint light revealed the monstrosity that was Borus, his massive shoulders marked by long horns of ivory. Borus wailed his gigantic arms to and fro, chasing something in the dark. Another cry pierced through the air, and Borus roared in pain.

A black jaguar had pounced upon Borus's chest, jaws locked onto the Minotaur's neck. Borus grasped the jaguar with its great hands. James's instincts finally jolted him into action. He dropped the lamp and surged toward Borus. Lowering his head and shoulders, he threw himself at Borus. He collided with it, tackling it around its torso. His momentum carried himself, Borus, and Quetzal into the darkness. They smashed into the cavern wall, and James fell to the ground after the collision. He was stunned, but he jumped back onto his feet. He flailed his arms in the blackness, and some of his blows struck Borus.

Borus howled as Quetzal's fangs remained plunged into its neck, and James continued to pummel it with his fists. The ivory horns upon Borus's shoulders had embedded themselves into the stone wall, and it struggled to pull itself free. Still, with a powerful sweep of its arm, Borus struck James across the face, sending the man soaring backwards through the air. James landed hard, striking his head against the ground. He forced himself up, but swayed dizzily. He stumbled towards the cries and grunts, knowing that he should persist. He *must* persist, or all was lost.

Hugar had come forth and traded blows with Borus, while Quetzal leapt in and out of the fray, pestering the indomitable beast with his claws and fangs. Just as Hugar was struck to the ground, James re-entered the fight, buffeting Borus in its side.

Even as blood gurgled in his throat, Hugar yelled out, "Don't stop. We must not stop!"

The three men knew that none of them could relent in their onslaught. If one of them would fall and not rebound, they would all fall. Through the endless minutes that followed, they endured through Borus's punishing blows; they persisted even when gored by his unforgiving horns. They flailed and kicked blindly, hoping to find Borus in the absolute darkness. Even as he was repeatedly punished, James felt a power surge within him. Adrenaline throbbed through his body, not only immunizing him from the lashing pain, but catalyzing a growing bloodlust that fueled his fists. As he sensed Borus losing strength, James increased his assault.

Finally, the behemoth slumped to his knees, and James pounced, erupting in a frightening frenzy of blows and rakes upon the body of Borus. In the stygian darkness, the great beast fell before his feet.

Chapter 18

The Honor of the Son

THE THREE BATTERED men trudged slowly toward the light of their remaining lamp. As they entered the illuminated sphere, they looked at each other. Hugar and James had both been gored by Borus and blood soaked their shirts. Quetzal was back in his human form, and he limped into the glow of the lamp behind the other two men. He hunched over, his hands on his knees, and coughed out blood, splattering the stone floor.

James could feel his wounds healing, although the pain increased as his adrenalized rage ebbed away. Hugar's face was bruised and swollen, his hair and beard matted with both his own blood and that of Borus.

"We slayed a Minotaur," Quetzal groaned.

"Indeed," said Hugar. "Never an easy task, especially underground and in the dark." He bent over and picked up the lamp. "Now, let's see what's behind the curtain."

They turned around and searched for the far end of the cavern. It was suddenly deathly quiet, and their footsteps echoed throughout the underground lair. They stood before the covering of branches that they discovered before Borus's attack. Hugar nodded at James, who stepped forward. With a sweep of his hand, he demolished the weakly tethered twigs. Beyond was an opening in the cavern wall. Hugar once again lifted the lamp.

Pale Echidna stared at them from the dark recess with sad gray eyes. The men drew sharp breaths, stunned by a passing moment of fear, as well by her ghostly beauty. She was seated on her coiled serpent tail, which looped and spiraled up and behind her torso, filling the small space. Her arms dangled to her sides.

The three men stared at her, waiting for her eyes to flicker, for her to suddenly awaken and attack, as Borus had done. Like dazed children, they stood for long moments. Her flesh looked gray and frosty, but it refused after four decades to succumb to decomposition. Their eyes lingered on the red stone embedded in the center of her forehead. An ever faint light pulsed in its core, barely perceptible.

"Go, James," Hugar finally whispered.

James edged forward, his gaze fixed on the great stone. He was mesmerized by it. Approaching lethargically, his right hand slowly rose toward Echidna's brow. This intimately close, he could see the subtle scaling of her skin, the oily texture that endured even so long after her death. He could see the forked tongue slightly protruding from between her purple, stippled lips.

His fingers reached Echidna's stone, and a finger slowly brushed against its dusty surface. Its inner light flared ever so slightly at his touch. He clawed at the stone's edges with his rough, untrimmed fingernails. Her skin smudged like wax as he dug into her brow, and he pried the stone out of her head.

He held the stone in his hand and glanced at her face. A dark cavity sat where the stone used to reside. Suddenly, her pupils, which had been a dull gray, faded away, and her eyes became only white slits in her head.

As he held the stone in his hand, the nausea overcame him, and his stomach clenched. He wretched and then turned to his two companions.

"James," called Quetzal, "are you sure you want to do this?"

Anger flashed across Hugar's face.

"Of course, he does," Hugar said. "His mother could be in there. You don't leave family behind to rot in something like that— a miniscule prison such as that!"

Quetzal looked concerned.

"Perhaps there's another way," he said.

"*Cállate!*" Hugar shouted. "*El necesita más corage, no tus comentarios absurdos!*"

James didn't understand Spanish, but he recognized it from his youth.

"*No hay otro camino para hacer esto?*" Quetzal blurted in response.

Hugar turned toward James. His eyes burned.

"Courage, James, conviction!" he exhorted. "Do you want to save your mother? Press the stone to your brow. Only one can save her, and that is you, my brother. Bring her back to the land of the living."

James brought the stone to his forehead. It was cold to the touch. The world lurched around him, and everything went dark.

Silence. The light from Hugar's lamp had melted away. James was standing, his arms to his side. The large gemstone was no longer in his hand.

"Hugar?" he whispered. "Quetzal?"

No answer came. His eyes adjusted to the dark. He could see faint outlines of walls on either side of him. He was in an unlit corridor. He walked forward. The corridor went for a long ways. He kept walking. More light began to seep into his field of vision. He was in a hallway. The flooring was wood. Paintings lined the walls, but it was too dark to see any details.

After some time, the hallway finally ended. Another corridor led to the left and the right. To the right, he could see a half-opened door at the far end. A faint light came from beyond the door. He turned towards it.

As he quietly walked, the warm yellow light illuminated more paintings. They were pictures of different people, some just portraits, and some were more elaborated paintings of people from different periods in history. One particular man, thin with sharp features, posed in different paintings in different styles of dress. James stopped at one particular painting. *I've seen this painting before*, he thought. In it, the thin man wore a feathered hat. He wore a doublet which came up and covered his entire neck. A white ruffled collar rose above the doublet and framed his jaw-line. The man was fair-skinned with brown eyes and dark hair.

He moved further down the hall. When he had nearly arrived at the door, he froze. His mother, Emilia Worth, gazed at him from the wall. It was a large photograph, in black and white, one that he had never seen before. She looked young, about twenty. She wore a long white dress and held a parasol. She was beaming. James had never seen his mother look so happy and beautiful.

He searched his pockets and pulled out the old yellowed photograph that Hugar gave to him. He looked at the photo in the dim light.

The door waited for him, a few feet away. The yellow light flickered gently from behind the half-opened door. His heart swelled and an inner music called to him from the room beyond. He walked through, brushing open the door.

He found a den lined with book shelves. On the shelves sat hundreds of leather-bound books. An old-fashioned candle lamp set in one wall lit the room with its lightly dancing flame. A small table stood surrounded by two velvet maroon chairs. He walked over to the table. A fine white teapot adorned with gold trim waited with two teacups. He lingered at the table.

A voice came from a corner: "Good evening, young Henry."

He looked at the shadowed corner. A figure emerged slowly from the dark corner. It was a man, not tall in stature. He sported a black smoking jacket and held a pipe casually between a pair of fingers. The smell from the pipe was an acrid herb James couldn't identify. The man's hair was white, and his beard was fuller, but James recognized him from all the paintings in the hallway.

"Who are you?" James asked.

The man smiled blandly.

"Maybe this would make matters more discernible," he said, raising his left arm towards the adjacent wall. The lone candle burned with more intensity, and a painting on the wall appeared in the light. James surveyed the painting. The man, wearing a black suit and white tie, stood in the image with his hands behind his back. Emilia, his mother, wearing a black gown as well as an insincere smile, stood next to the man. She was holding a baby in her arms.

James took a step back. He reached out to one of the chairs for support.

"I'm your father," the man said with a slow nod of the head. "Honus Roosevelt. So pleased to see you again."

James's knees buckled. He clutched the back of the chair. The nausea he felt earlier in the cavern, as he held the gem—it was the same revulsion he experienced in the home of Amargat. It was the sickness he felt when holding the stone imbued with a memory of his father.

The red gemstone of Echidna harbored his father.

"Please son, sit down," Honus said.

Honus waited for him to fall back into the chair, and then sat down across from him.

"Where is … my mother?" James asked.

"Emilia. She is not here," Honus answered. He lifted the teapot. "Some tea?"

"No, thank you," James said.

"Please, I insist," Honus said. "It'll help with your vertigo."

Honus poured some tea for the both of them, and then took his cup and sipped.

"It's not real, in any case," Honus said, "the tea, nor any of these other trappings—the chair, the paintings, the rooms, and hallways. But it helps to pass the time, and to fend off the mania."

James raised his eyes to his father's.

"You're real," he said.

"Yes," said Honus. "I am real. And so are you, James Henry. To my greatest contentment and pride, you are bona fide, and you are in front of me at long last."

Honus took some time to observe James, continuing to sip on his tea.

"You know, I suggested the name 'Henry,'" he said. "I am quite fond of names starting with the letter 'H' and also insisted that you take your mother's surname. More inconspicuous that way, but alas it didn't matter in the end. Now, 'James'—that was Emilia's choice. She was quite enamored with the writer Henry James, and always said she related to his character, Daisy Miller. She enjoyed reading, your mother. My opinion is, why read about life, when you can live it." He paused. "Look at me, shameful, carrying on and on with my special guest."

"So where is Mother?" James interjected.

"She's long gone, unfortunately."

"What do you mean by that?"

"I mean," said Honus, "that she is dead."

The revelation hit him in the gut. Some of the rage from earlier returned, and he stood up.

"This is your fault!" he shouted. He rushed forward at his father.

Honus barely lifted a finger and a cylindrical barrier appeared around James. He crashed against it. It was translucent, with a slight bluish hue. He pounded against it with a fist, but it was impervious.

"I understand your anger," Honus said. "And I expected it."

"Let me out of here!" James yelled.

"This is for your own good," Honus said. "You don't expect me to joust with my own son, do you?"

James hammered at the barrier, but it was no use. His energy and anger dissipated, and he slumped against it.

"Do you know who is really responsible for your pain?" asked Honus.

"Your wife, Margaret," James spat. "But where were you when they tortured me? When they killed my mother!"

"She's a clever one, Margaret. She immured me here long before she touched you or Emilia. But she managed to let me know, even when I was trapped in this forsaken prison, what she was doing. Please understand, son, I am her victim, also."

With another flick of his finger, Honus removed the barrier. James wavered where he stood, and then he slumped back into the chair.

"Have a drink," Honus said. "You'll feel better."

James drank, and he began to feel better. His muscles loosened. The anger subsided.

"There, there," said Honus. "Better, isn't it?"

"Yes."

"Well, my son, you have finally met your father. Doesn't this rouse any curiosity within you? This is our opportunity to become acquainted."

James still found himself gripping the armrest a bit tightly.

"Is it true?" he asked. "Did she do this out of jealousy?"

"Well, I confess," Honus said, "I wronged her. I sullied her reputation, by siring you."

"You mean by cheating on her."

"Yes, if that is the word you must use."

"Mother was just some woman you had an affair with."

"You speak like the mortals. Why must you join them in trivializing these matters which are so much more complex than—"

"And you are so much better?" James interrupted. "Because you're some sort of angel, you can just go around ruining people's lives? My life?"

"Mind your tongue, young man," Honus replied, his eyes suddenly cold. "I see that Hugar has kept much of it from you. So it is I who must choose now how much to reveal."

Honus stood up, and he walked to the far end of the room. He pulled a curtain aside on the far wall. Some moonlight spilled into the room. He stayed at the window for a long while, staring sullenly into the distance. James looked around the room again. He examined the painting of his father, his mother, and himself. It melted into darkness intermittently. As he focused on the details around him, he noticed those details flickered in and out of perception.

Tired, he sat down on the floor and leaned back against a wall of books. One of the leather-bound books fell off of a shelf. He gathered it in his hands. On the front cover, a simple image of a mountain was burned into the surface of the leather.

"*Har Hermon*," Honus said. "Or Mount Hermon in your language. You are welcome to peruse its contents, although I doubt you read Aramaic or Hebrew."

James opened the book. Indeed, the curving, undulating script was mere scribbling to him.

"I have decided to enlighten you," Honus said. "Bear in mind that this is a vast departure from custom. Hugar did not know anything until he was past three centuries old. Even then, he was very young."

James put the book down and listened.

"I am, or once was, one of the *Benei Ha'Elohim*. Have you ever heard that phrase?"

"No, never."

"It is Hebrew, but no matter, we are known by different names in different corners of the world—words in different tongues meaning titans, gods. Our children, in an older time, were called heroes, giants, *Nephilim*, or even gods themselves."

"I have been told some of this," interrupted James. "You are one of the Watchers, whatever that means."

"Ah yes, that is another one of our names—*Irin*, or Watchers. Let's stay with the title of Watcher, may we? Two hundred of us were assigned on earth to oversee the smatterings of humans. Over many tens of thousands of years, the humans multiplied, their societies developed, slowly. We watched. After a long period, we came to believe that the rich lands of the earth were being wasted on indolent and incoherent men. The daughters of men had allure, but we began to wonder why the pitiable humans were given free roam of the earth. And why we were helping them to do so.

"Meeting upon Mount Hermon, we pledged our devotion to each other, our unity in cause. The ones who had watched would take the earth for our own! We went north. We flaunted our strength. Before us, chieftains and warriors either bowed to us or lay slain. Their most beautiful daughters we took as our wives. And then, we shared our knowledge with our subjects. We would instruct and equip them. We nurtured within them a lust for conquest that would drive them north, south, east, and west.

"Oh, how our comrade, *Azâzêl*, threw himself into his mission with such prodigious passion. He taught the men to draw metals from the earth and fashion them into swords and shields. He demonstrated how to craft the metal also into bracelets and adornments. *Azâzêl* instilled in the women the art of using coloring tinctures and how to embellish their eyelids. Grand, obstinate *Azâzêl* —he was enamored with both war and beauty."

Honus's eyes glimmered in the candle light. He stood in the middle of the room, telling his story with hands raised. His voice had risen as he spoke of the Watchers, but now he trembled slightly as he lowered his hands.

"I've also heard of *Azâzêl*," James said. "He, you, and Amargat are all Watchers, right?"

"We were," Honus said. "There are no more Watchers."

"What happened?" asked James.

"I, Amargat, and four others, we saw the folly of our plot. We were distressed by the education given to these tribes in the north. As they spread and conquered, our conviction against this path grew. Generations passed, and soon the ancestors of these original tribes turned their greedy eyes to the Holy Lands in the south."

Honus, tears now beginning to flow down his wrinkled face, looked at James. His eyes pleaded for understanding.

"We had no choice," Honus whispered. "Six of us decided to betray our comrades, our brothers. We sought out our former *Sar*, who had commanded us. We colluded with him, bringing about the downfall of our brothers. *Azâzêl* was cast into the earth to spend this age being ravaged by an eagle of the depths. Our actions brought about the demise of most of our children. Those children that remained, they eventually passed away and were forgotten. And the six betrayers ... we received no thanks for saving this wretched world. We have since rotted here amongst the mortals. We lived in fear and remorse. We spurned siring more children. We endured alone, with no sons and daughters to serve us."

"But you do have children," countered James. "Me, Hugar, Zachary, and Charlotte. How many more are there?"

"True. You see, one of the six finally gathered enough courage to raise child once again. Margaret was the first since the rebellion was crushed. After her birth, we waited. We anticipated retribution from the heavens, but none came. Soon, more children were born. Margaret's sister, Helena, Hugar. It was arranged that I would marry Margaret, and our children would signal a new era. We would make this world ours again, quietly.

"At the beginning of the 20th century, most of the six came to the United States. We abandoned our former names. I chose my present name, 'Honus,' after a renowned athlete at the time—a baseball player if I recall correctly, and my surname, 'Roosevelt,' after the president of the United States."

He smiled. "We had grand ambitions. But, as fate would have it, Margaret could not bear us children. We tried for a sufficient time, but we did not succeed. This devastated her. She turned to sorcery to correct her affliction, but nothing worked. To make matters worse, her younger sister, Helena, had also been paired with another of the fallen six.

"Amargat," James said. "I have met him."

"Have you?" asked Honus. "He can be quite prickly, but a very capable and sensible brother-in-arms. He and Helena waited centuries to allow Margaret to mourn and accept her inability to bear children. But it wasn't enough. When Helena became pregnant, Margaret was enraged. She was insufferable. This was when she became entirely engrossed in the dark arts. I am the only one who knows this, but she placed a curse on Helena. When Helena bore Zachary and Charlotte, she died in the birthing process— "

Honus paused, and he grimaced at the memory.

"Through the curse, Margaret entrapped Helena's soul. In a terrible ceremony, she transformed Helena into a beast."

"A Minotaur!" cried out James.

"Yes," Honus said. "One that I assume you defeated to arrive at this juncture."

"And you got my mother involved with this madwoman?"

"It was never my intention. I acquired a house on the West Coast. This was my retreat, away from business, and away from Margaret. Your mother, as kind as she was, came by to welcome her new neighbor. I was stricken by her, and I must admit, I was in a … vulnerable state at that point in time."

Vulnerable? James gritted his teeth.

"James, I did love your mother. You were born a few years after Zachary and Charlotte. Emilia moved into the house I had bought, and I vowed to stay away, for your own protection. I knew that if Margaret ever found out—" He stopped. He put his smoking pipe in his mouth, and after a moment he muttered, "Well, she did, and you saw what happened."

"My mother is dead," said James.

Honus walked back to the window, pulling aside a curtain to look outside. He smoked from his pipe, content that the story was done. The two men waited a while, having nothing more to say to each other.

"So what now?" James eventually asked. "Can Hugar and Quetzal get us out of here?"

"Quetzal?" Honus said. He was slightly startled.

"Yes, Quetzal. He works for Hugar."

Honus thought a moment.

"You must mean," he said, "*Mahin*. He is another of my sons."

James recognized the name. He thought back to Quetzal's story about Dona Marina.

"Mahin, he finally came to find me, to be reunited," Honus beamed. "You see, my son, this is the destiny of the children, the *Nephilim*. You are not immortal. You will not live into eternity. So what greater purpose is there than to serve your fathers? In that way, your imprint will last forever."

Honus wrapped his arms around himself, and bowed his head. "I have carried a memory with me for thousands of years," he said. "Before sending us on our way, our *Sar* gave each of the six a prophecy. These prophecies were to be the last command we would ever receive from the heavens."

"What was your prophecy?" James asked.

"That I would be saved in my most dire moment, by one that I had sired," Honus said.

"You would be saved by one of your sons?" James asked, standing up.

"Hugar is my eldest. He is my most loyal servant, and I knew he would find a way to save me. This prison was no place for one of the *Benei Ha'Elohim*, even one who was rejected. But he has sent you to perform an honored duty, a fine sacrifice. This is what we swore to on Mt. Hermon—that our sons and daughters would serve us in our will."

"I don't know what you're talking about," James said. "I came here to find my mother. That's it." He looked at his father and took a hesitant step forward. But the room was already darkening. The books and table faded away. Everything faded away. Honus was stepping backwards.

"Thank you, my son," Honus said. "You have achieved your greatest glory. You have assisted Hugar in liberating me. Never forget that."

Then his father turned around and disappeared into the growing darkness. James chased after him. He grasped in the dark. He sprinted forward. He searched to his right and to his left. He listened, and he strained his eyes to see something, anything. But it was no use. There was nothing. Absolutely nothing.

Chapter 19

Nothing and Everything

HALLUCINATIONS CAREENED around him. In the total absence of light and sound, an infinite array of sensations danced in and around the nothingness. Stray thoughts echoed through the vastness and bounced back, metamorphosed into amplified nightmares. He floated through a universe with no stars. He was asleep, but always awake. He was wide awake, but always in slumber.

He would often reach out and touch his own arm, or put his hands on his face, to remind himself that he was a man, to remind himself that he was once a person with a living body. He would curl up like a child in bed, or a fetus in the womb. He would stretch out arms and legs and reach to touch something, but absolutely nothing was there. He would scream until his lungs burned, but the sound of his voice never returned to his ears. He sang silent songs.

He existed as such for some length of time. He searched for something that was always on the edge of his consciousness. He knew it was there. It scratched his mind, but it eluded him. He decided to stop searching for it, and instead asked for it to come to him. He asked politely. It revealed itself as a point of dull gray in the far distance, almost indistinguishable even in the severe black of his universe. He focused on it and asked it softly to come to him.

The sphere approached him slowly, and he waited patiently. As it neared, a soft light uncloaked his being, illuminating his hands and arms. He looked about him and saw his torso, still wrapped in a shirt that he remembered from long ago. The fabric rippled about his body as it was buffeted by a new wind. *Gravity*. He was falling. He was falling toward the growing point of gray.

"Gently," he whispered. *Sound*.

His descent slackened. The thing he searched for approached him, a perfectly solemn face. He landed softly on the small globe of dusty stone, suspended in his starless universe. He looked about. Its diameter was no more than two lengths of his body. He sat and looked out into the blackness.

"Stars," he whispered, delighting in the sound of his voice.

Tiny points of light slowly twinkled into existence.

"More."

The points of light multiplied and scattered throughout his universe. He stood up on his minuscule planet and laughed and clapped at the performance of the stars.

He hesitantly stepped forward, and gravity kept him standing on solid ground. He kneeled to the ground and traced in the dust, "I am who?" He said the words out loud.

He walked his little earth, but within seconds he had come back to his words in the ground.

"Bigger," he whispered.

The tiny planet rumbled, and then it grew. It expanded and quaked until he could no longer see the curve of the horizon. He walked his dusty planet as the stars revolved above him. Around and around they spun over his head. He searched for something new, but for a long time, he didn't know what he sought, for he had forgotten of things such as the sun, home, and friends.

After his stars had traversed the sky many times, the memory of the sun emerged in his mind. He painted it rising from the far horizon, and then so arrived also the memory of east and west, north and south. He basked in the new warmth of the world.

When his sun retreated farther into the sky, and the world once again became cold, he finally remembered home. He walked west and found the boundary of land and water. In this land of crashing waves and sandy shore, he summoned a house which erupted from the depths of the earth. He walked through its doors and thought it had a familiar smell.

And, he was no longer alone. As he wandered from room to room, he would find others. They lingered in rooms when he paid no attention but kept their backs turned and their eyes elsewhere. He would follow them but they would walk into hallways or closets and disappear. He stalked the apparitions until one by one, he remembered their names. *Hugar. Quetzal. Amos. Rhiannon.* These names came to him easiest.

One day, he followed an apparition into the kitchen. She waited for him, sitting at the small dining table. He looked at her face.

"Your name … is Emilia," he said.

"You can call me Mom," she smiled.

"Mom. Yes, you're my mother."

"I bore you. I fed you. I loved you and tried to raise you right."

"Are you proud, Mom? Did you raise me right?"

She grimaced, and tears rolled down her cheeks.

"I had you for such a short time," she said. "I don't think you remember me."

"I … remember you."

"Good," she said, wiping her eyes with a handkerchief. "I don't care what your father was. Don't forget, I'm your mother. You're just as much me, on the outside, as you are him. And on the inside, you're all my doing. And I'm so proud."

She stood up and gave him one last smile before hurrying from the room.

On another day, when the sun was descending in his sky, he was lying in the hammock in the backyard. A cloud appeared over the yard, and down jumped a Minotaur.

The Minotaur approached him and then leaned against one of the trees. It broke off a twig from the tree and began to pick at its sharp, ugly teeth.

"Howdy, I'm Borus," it said in a deep voice.

"I remember you. Isn't your real name Helena?"

"Yes, that may be true," the Minotaur answered after thinking for a long while. "I bested you once, didn't I? And then you defeated me in turn."

"I had the help of two friends."

"Were they really your friends?" the Minotaur asked.

"At that time, yes."

"I would say, they were never your friends."

"Then you're wiser than me."

"No, I only know as much as you do."

The Minotaur would appear now and then, often when he was lying in that hammock.

But mostly, the days were empty, and visitors were few. He began to remember the old world that existed beyond his sky. He would stare up into his perfect blue sky, and just beyond the boundary of sight, he would perceive a red shell. His crystal prison.

The memories continued to reveal themselves. He had been betrayed by family. He was a pawn and a sacrifice. He kept this new pain inside, but it bubbled and thrashed about in his gut.

One day, when the sun was high overhead, he stood in front of his house and let out a great roar. His anger boiled, and the house exploded in flames. He yelled until it was a smoldering heap.

He collapsed to the ground and turned onto his back to watch the sky redden. There were no more blue skies. Dark clouds hid the sun at day, and at night, he watched the stars journey ever so slowly above him.

"You are my stars of destiny," he whispered to them every night. "My hopeless fate."

During the plentiful nights, he crafted and recited these words to them, his only audience:

> You are my stars of Destiny
> My hopeless Fate
> When my life is wrested from me
> On that faraway date
> While all that lived, burns around me
> End my memories
> While I lie on the smoldering heap
> End my centuries
> Never a mark have I left behind
> Only a fool was I
> Devil's work and Angel's crime
> Only a pawn was I
> I say shelter not and rescue not
> What isn't of worth
> Fate already written and Destiny taught
> For this James Henry Worth

So there he lay, day after night, and night after day. And he enjoyed the nights more, for he had the constellations. During the day, the red sky reminded him of his prison. But during the nights, he counted the stars.

Then came a night, when a strange thing occurred. A new star bloomed, and before his very eyes, it fell from the sky. As a meteor blazing from the heavens, it came silently, and it landed nearby.

It landed to the east, where the sun used to rise, and he peered toward that horizon, for hours until the stars said good-bye. The sky once again reddened, and the clouds grumbled overhead. Off in the distance, he saw someone. As the person came closer, he saw it was a man walking slowly. For the first time in a long while, an apparition had come to visit. James stood up as the man approached. Taking off his hat, the man revealed blond hair, and sad blue eyes.

"Hello, Jimmy," the man said.

James squinted. It was his old friend, Amos. He was older, with stubble on his chin and cheeks. His eyes were filled with sorrow, his jaw tense with regret.

"Well, hi there, Amos."

Amos looked around.

"So this is your dream world," he said. "It's pretty bleak."

"Dream world?" James asked.

"Yeah, I've talked to—well, never mind," Amos said.

"You're not how I remember you."

"It's been a while," he said. "Things change."

"I had a house here," James said, nodding toward the black plot of earth. "I could raise another but I don't feel like it."

"It's alright. Listen, you don't belong here, anyhow."

"Why not? I have my place. I have my stars."

Amos tilted his head a bit. He took a good look at James.

"I'm sorry, Jimmy," Amos said. "It's my fault you're here. I never should have let you go get this cursed gem."

James needed a few moments to remember this part of his past.

"Ah yes, I came to find my mother," he said. "I found my father instead."

"Yes, I know," Amos said. "I knew more than I let on. I was working for Hugar, remember? Your half-brother had been looking for your father for a long time. I was pretty sure that's what you were going to find, and I was right."

James paused for a while. "No matter," he finally said. "Would you like for me to conjure anything up for you, before you disappear?"

"What?" responded Amos. "No, no, Jimmy I'm not going anywhere. You are."

"I'm not going anywhere. This is my home. This is my tomb."

James reached with a hand towards the ground. He lifted his hand and a batch of the dark earth rose from the ground and into the sky. With a flick of a finger, the dirt dispersed on the wind. He looked into the newly-made hole in the ground. A coffin materialized, and its lid sprang open. White silk lined its interior.

Amos looked at the coffin, and he dropped to his knees.

"You can't stay, Jimmy," he pleaded. "We've done a terrible thing, letting your father free."

Amos began to sob. James closed the lid of the coffin with another flick of his finger. He leapt across to his friend's side.

"What are you saying?" he asked.

"I'm here to stay," Amos said. "I'm trapped here, just as you became trapped here when you arrived. You're free to go."

A deep rumble sounded from the earth. James looked around. He noticed that the color at the horizon was bleeding away. The earth trembled slightly beneath his feet.

"Your dream, this world, it's falling apart," Amos said. "You can see it, even as I speak."

The sky was cracking open, revealing pure darkness. The earth's quaking became louder and more violent. In the distance, he could see entire sections of the landscape collapsing.

"What am I supposed to do?" James blurted.

"Just let this world go," Amos responded. "She'll be waiting for you, on the other side."

"Rhiannon?"

"Yes, please take care of her. Maybe you can undo some of what I've done."

The ground was now shaking tremendously under James's feet. The two men had to shout to be heard above the din of the world coming to an end. Amos cringed as he looked around at the universe he had entered.

"Amos, listen!" James shouted. "Have no fear. When the world goes to black, start from the beginning."

"What do you mean?" Amos shouted in return.

"Create, start from nothing. Gravity, sound, light. Be brave, and I will come back for you!"

The ground beneath James gave way, and he fell into the depths.

Amos remained. The land all around him continued to collapse. The color of the world seeped away, and blackness encroached. Amos trembled as the darkness engulfed him.

James was plunging through a black void. Soon, a light appeared. It cut through time and space and bathed him. Then, he was no longer falling. He was rising in a sea of white light. The light slowly began to dissipate, and lines and colors began to emerge.

He heard a faraway voice calling his name, and then a woman began to fade into view. He admired the lines of her eyes, her face, as her image broke through the white glare. A soft breeze brushed against his skin, and he began to smell earth and grass.

He sensed the world laid out before him, and he stepped into it. It was not yet his end.

Look for the second book in the *Son of the Fallen* series,
coming in 2012.

More information at: http://www.alantluu.com
Twitter: http://www.twitter.com/alanluu
Email: alanluu@live.com

About the Author

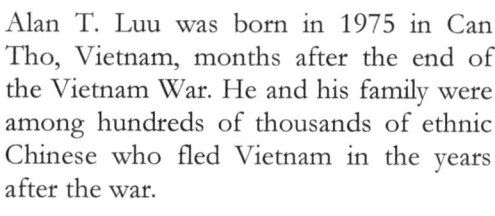

Alan T. Luu was born in 1975 in Can Tho, Vietnam, months after the end of the Vietnam War. He and his family were among hundreds of thousands of ethnic Chinese who fled Vietnam in the years after the war.

They were fortunate enough to be accepted as refugees into the United States, where Alan would start kindergarten without a lick of English ability. Years later, he would become a naturalized U.S. citizen and graduate from UCLA with a B.A. in Sociology.

Along the way, Alan discovered a love for the arts, including dance, theater, and of course, writing. He currently lives in Germany with his new wife and is excited to share the first book in his series, SON OF THE FALLEN.

www.ingramcontent.com/pod-product-compliance
Lightning Source LLC
Chambersburg PA
CBHW050938120626
46552CB00001B/271